•

SERIAL
KILLER
DAYS

•

Also by David Prill

The Unnatural

A Novel by
David Prill

•

SERIAL KILLER DAYS

•

St. Martin's Press
New York

SERIAL KILLER DAYS. Copyright © 1996 by David Prill. All rights reserved. Printed in the United States of America. No part of this book may be used or reproduced in any manner whatsoever without written permission except in the case of brief quotations embodied in critical articles or reviews. For information, address St. Martin's Press, 175 Fifth Avenue, New York, N.Y. 10010.

Edited by Gordon Van Gelder
Design by Pei Loi Koay

Library of Congress Cataloging-in-Publication Data

Prill, David.
        Serial killer days / by David Prill.
              p.   c.m.
        ISBN 0-312-14411-3
        I. Title.
    PS3566.R568S47   1996
    813'.54—dc20   96-6874
                                          CIP

First edition: June 1996

10   9   8   7   6   5   4   3   2   1

CIVIC
DUTIES

1

Debbie Morning woke up happy.

I reckon there's never been a morning as lovely as this one, she thought, sliding out of bed and going to her second-floor window. The sun had shinnied up the trees on the east edge of town and was looking for her. She pulled apart the white curtains and let it in. Hello sun, bless you for stopping by. Oh, and the sky is so blue today, if it's been a bluer blue I can't recall when. Yesterday it was quite blue, but today I must say it is very, very blue. Many a poem has been inspired by a sky like that. Then Debbie saw Mrs. Grackle on a branch in the big box elder tree at the edge of the yard, and waved a greeting. You're looking well today, ma'am. The grackle squawked, and Debbie thought, You're welcome.

Debbie made her bed, careful to smooth out all the wrinkles in the bedspread, the one with the spiraling, grinning suns on a field of blue, her most favorite of all her bedspreads, although she certainly loved her other bedspreads as well, particularly the one with the smiling kitties, which were not spiraling but were grinning as they played with a ball of bright blue yarn.

Sitting down in front of the mirror, Debbie brushed her long blonde hair, counting off the strokes in a singsong voice: "one, two, three, four, . . . thirty-two." Thirty-two was not her favorite number. She had nothing against thirty-two, not really, but if she had a choice she would have picked another number, like eighteen, her age, or four, her birthday. But thirty-two it had to be because she had tried thirty-one and it made her hair look like she hadn't even bothered to brush it, and she had tried thirty-three and that was the point when her hair would get all electrified. That one extra stroke made a huge difference. So she stuck with thirty-two, and actually was pretty happy about it.

Keeping an eye on the clock, Debbie brushed her teeth, washed her face, and got dressed, putting on her Standard Springs High Cheer Squad T-shirt and jeans. Her throat was still a little coarse from last week, but she expected it would get better once she warmed up. Mrs. Toddler was expecting her to arrive for practice at 9:00 a.m. sharp, and it would not do to show up late, especially with the pageant so few days away. She tugged on her sneakers, double-knotting them to avoid the risk of a lace coming untied, grabbed her book, and headed downstairs.

"Morning, Mother, little brother," said Debbie. She poured herself a glass of Florida sunshine and sat down at the breakfast table, where Bobby was stabbing at his grapefruit. She tousled his blond crew cut. "I've got to run in a minute. Don't want to be late for practice!"

Her mother, a small woman with curly blonde hair, came close, her dark, swollen eyes studying her carefully. "How are you feeling today, dear?"

"Great, Mom! How are you?"

"Did you have any bad dreams?"

"No. Wait a sec, yes I did!"

"You did?" Mother asked, her pasty face brightening. "You really did?"

"Yes. I dreamed I was eating an apple and there was a bug in it."

"Bugs, that's good."

"I ate a bug yesterday!" Bobby chimed in.

"It was just one bug, Mom."

"A big one?"

"Not too big."

"Were you afraid?"

"Well, it was just a little bug."

"Did it have a stinger?"

"No, he had a very kind face."

Shoulders slumping, her mother sat down and buttered a slice of toast, saying, "Well, you have a good day, dear. Listen closely to Mrs. Toddler. She's been to Paris, you know. In France they would call her an artiste."

"I like her, Mom. I always listen to her." Debbie took a big gulp of her juice and jumped up. "See you later!"

As she was leaving, her mom called out, "Debbie, could you stop by the butcher shop on the way home and get a ham hock? I want to make soup tonight."

"Sure thing!" Debbie said brightly and skedaddled out the door.

I sure wish Mom wouldn't worry about me so much, Debbie thought as she walked briskly up Vine Street, skipping around the spray of the sprinklers that crept through the shady, well-tended yards. I know this is my last chance in the pageant, but I have faith that things will work out this time, especially after coming so close last year. All that extra practice I put in over the winter will pay off, I'm sure it will.

Their neighbors, the Gears, were busy touching up their house, repainting the big red x's on the doors and around the windows. Mr. Gear was on the ladder, sweeping a brush across the second-story window, their remaining child's bedroom. Debbie used to baby-sit for them, not so much anymore.

"Morning, Mr. and Mrs. Gear!" Debbie called out, slowing to a stroll.

Mr. Gear, in suspenders and jack boots, looked over his shoulder and waved with his paintbrush hand. Down below, spots of red dotted Mrs. Gear's white blouse. "Hon, be careful with that. I just washed this blouse." Mrs. Gear flapped her hand at Debbie. "Good morning, dear. A lovely day, isn't it?"

"Oh, it's the best," Debbie replied. "Did you happen to notice how blue the sky is today?"

"Why, no," she said, craning her neck. "It *is* quite blue, isn't it?"

"You could write a poem about it, if you wanted to." Debbie resumed her pace. "Have a nice day!"

Mrs. Toddler's house, a big, saltine box, New England–looking affair, was set at the end of Vine Street, right beside a pond with cattails and bullfrogs and water lilies and dragonflies and crickets and so many other wonderful things. Debbie liked to sit on the big white rock at the pond's edge and listen to the bullfrogs sing. Sometimes she sang along.

Debbie headed up the sidewalk to the steps with the year 1924 stenciled into the mottled concrete. She went in the porch and knocked on the front door. Moments later she heard the floor creaking and then the door swung open.

"Hi, Mrs. Toddler. I'm not late, am I?"

"Right on time as usual," the older woman said with a smile. "Come in."

Mrs. Toddler always looked so elegant. Even at nine o'clock on a Friday morning, she was dressed in a black chenille evening gown, set off nicely by her flowing white hair and a strand of pearls.

"Did you get that dress in France?" Debbie asked, moving a burgundy-and-gold Niagara Falls pillow as she sat down on the couch. She set her book on the end table.

"No, I bought this in Paristown, up in Larry County."

Paristown. That was where *he* lived. Debbie sighed, then said, "I like it very much."

"Not quite appropriate for the pageant, though."

"No, of course not."

Mrs. Toddler tipped a teapot on the coffee table, filling a china cup. "Take a sip of hot lemon tea before we commence," she said, handing the cup to Debbie. "You sound a little hoarse. Have you been sleeping with the window open again?"

Debbie grinned sheepishly. She took a drink, shutting her

eyes as the hot liquid streamed down her throat. "Mmm. That feels much better."

"Let's begin, shall we?"

Mrs. Toddler took her place at the piano, Debbie standing alongside, clasping her hands at her waist. The teacher began playing, softly at first, almost like a lullaby, and Debbie weaved slightly, feeling the rhythm of the music, awaiting her cue. Then the music started on a crescendo, Mrs. Toddler nodded, and Debbie Morning began screaming. . . .

●

"That's fine," Mrs. Toddler said after the first section. "How does your throat feel?"

"I don't feel hoarse at all," replied Debbie. "I knew I just needed to get warmed up."

"Now, continue."

"AAAIIEEEEE! . . . UNH . . . WAIIIIII! . . ."

"He's coming to get you, Debbie! He's right behind you! He's about to grab you around the throat!"

"AIIIEEEEE! . . ."

When the piece had ended, Mrs. Toddler patted the keyboard cover, looking straight ahead, and said quietly, "We need to have a talk, my dear."

"Sure. What about?"

The mentor turned on the bench, and gazed at Debbie searchingly. "What do you think about when you're screaming?"

"Think about? Oh, I don't know. I was thinking about the new Rimbaud book I bought, working on the float tomorrow, Roger dear, ham hocks."

"Ham hocks?"

"Dinner."

"I see."

"My mind wanders, I guess."

Taking her hand, Mrs. Toddler said, "Now Debbie, you realize that this is your last chance to be Queen, don't you? That if you don't win this year you'll never walk down that aisle, no flowers, no crown, no chair of honor in the parade? You are simply not screaming with conviction. You aren't concentrating. Do you want to be on the ground floor of the float with the runner-ups like all the other years? Do you want Molly Lovey to win again? Although I've always felt that Molly has a certain superficial sense of terror that she brings to her screaming, I must say that I have on occasion got a sprinkling of gooseflesh after hearing her in full shriek."

Gooseflesh, Debbie thought with a twinge of envy.

"However, I also felt that you had an inner fear that we could bring out. Now I'm beginning to wonder. Aren't you afraid of *anything,* Debbie?"

"Well, Mrs. Toddler," Debbie said proudly, "if you must know I had a nightmare last night."

"Really? That's good. You should think about it while you're screaming. What was it about?"

"Bugs. Lots of big, black bugs crawling all over an apple I was about to eat. They had stingers and everything!"

"That's wonderful, dear." Mrs. Toddler smiled with obvious relief. "How is the violin practice coming?"

"Oh, I changed my mind about that," said Debbie. "Ole Rimbaud just put out a new book! *A Season in Heck.* I bought it yesterday. I haven't decided which selection to read."

This news appeared to dismay the mentor. "Now, my dear, I thought we had resolved this weeks ago. Judges aren't bowled over by poetry readings. Maybe Poe, but only if you dressed in black and threw a little blood around. But Rimbaud, Rimbaud . . . he's not frightening, he's depressing. There's no raw fear there, just angst and despair."

"But it's very fearful!" Debbie protested. "Here, I'll read some to you." She retrieved the small black book from the table. Flipping through the volume, she found her spot and said, "This one's called, 'Once, If I Recollect Right.'

"'Once, if I recollect right,'" she recited, "'my life was a Sun day dinner with all the fixins, where every heart said howdy, where every brewski flowed!

"'One night I gave Beauty a big ol' hug—and she didn't feel too swell, and I called her some sort of four-letter word. My hope has shriveled up like a prune. With a hop like a tomcat, I have caught and strangled every joy!

"'I will tear the curtains from every mystery—mysteries of religion or hog farmin' or what have you . . .'"

It was always a difficult choice to decide which poem to use in the talent competition. This year it was even more the case because the heralded hog farmer and decadent impressionist poet from Paristown, Minnesota, had been especially prolific, producing not one but two volumes of verse: *A Season in Heck,* which she had just read from, and *Delirium in the House of Swine.* For some reason he apparently had more free time this past year. Maybe, Debbie speculated, he had sold enough copies of the previous season's opus, *Paristown Bonfire,* to hire a boy to help out with the chores.

"I don't see how the judges can resist this time," Debbie told her mentor.

"Will you at least wear black?" Mrs. Toddler asked with resignation.

"You should see my gown," Debbie said with a proud smile.

Rising, the teacher said, measuring Debbie carefully with her eyes, "There is one other way. It's not guaranteed, I don't know how it will affect you, but we may want to consider it if your chances look bleak."

"What are you talking about?" asked Debbie, curious and a bit puzzled.

"I have a cousin, Gussie, who lives on Route Three north of town. She's a little odd, but she may be able to help you with your fear."

"What can she do?"

Shaking her head, Mrs. Toddler took Debbie's arm and led her to the door. "Let me give it some thought. Come back on Monday and we'll talk again. And make sure and rest that voice of yours!"

On the way home, Debbie cut down Bludgeon Street, which would take her to Main Street and the butcher shop. Passing by a pink house choked with ivy on the corner of Vine and Bludgeon, Debbie stopped, hearing the screams.

They were coming from Molly Lovey's house, the bedroom window wide open. She was practicing. Debbie stood there in the sun listening, her thin hand clenched white around her book. The screams were deep throated, wailing, each one fully fifteen seconds in length. Quite suddenly, goose bumps popped up along the length of Debbie's forearm. Frowning, she thought: That big phony! She probably left her window open on purpose, just to show off, to impress any judges that might be walking by. She's a big fake, probably not even scared at all, nobody can be that afraid. I can scream better than her any day of the week! Biting her lip, Debbie raced down the street, running until the screams faded and her skin returned to its smooth, unblemished state.

Going into town, Debbie could see that the preparations for next week were already well under way. City workers, precariously suspended in midair on apple pickers, were hanging oversize inflatable knives and handguns from the street lamps. Blood was running in the streets; the workers were testing the pump shooting out the nontoxic colored water that would heighten the mood on parade night. Merchants were placing colorful sale signs in their windows in anticipation of the big crowds that would be arriving next week.

And there, on the corner of Main and Pain, the locus of the parade route, they were stringing up the big black banner that announced: SERIAL KILLER DAYS—JULY 17–21.

Debbie grinned, basking in the warm memories of childhood. She remembered her dad waking her up in the middle of the night so they could go watch the Parade of Fear. She recalled the midway, the wonderful rides, could never keep her off the Scary-Go-Round. And most of all, the crowning of the Scream Queen. How frightened they all looked!

Now Debbie felt like her old self again. She put Molly Lovey out of her mind. After picking up the ham hock, she headed home with a skip in her step, feeling like an eight-year-old girl with her hair in pigtails. She couldn't help it. After all, Serial Killer Days was just around the corner. . . .

2

When Debbie arrived back at home, Mother was cutting up vegetables for the soup, while Junior hovered nearby, catching the odd carrot slice in his mouth as it scooted off the counter and peppering the cook with questions.

"Is he coming tonight? Is he coming tonight?" Bobby kept asking.

"No, not tonight, dear. Not for a few days yet. You'll just have to wait."

"The ham hock is in the building!" Debbie cheerfully announced.

"But I *can't* wait!"

"Just drop it in the pot, Debbie Sue."

Unwrapping the hock, Debbie carefully let it slide into the big brass kettle on the stove. It made a minor splash, slopping a dollop of water onto the floor and her T-shirt.

"How did practice go?"

"Well, Mother, if you must know," said Debbie, blotting her shirt with a dish towel and wiping the floor dry, "Mrs. Toddler said I have inner fear."

"*Inner* fear," her mother repeated proudly. "That's *very* nice."

"Say, Mom, do you know Mrs. Toddler's cousin Gussie? She lives north of town."

"Went to school with her. She got expelled for swinging a dead cat in the middle of math class while speaking in tongues. I never had much to do with her, if you must know. Why do you ask?"

"Oh, no reason, really," said Debbie, turning up the heat on the burner. "Mrs. Toddler just mentioned her. I had never heard of her."

Little Bobby tugged on his mother's arm. "Tell me the story again! I want to hear the story!"

"What story is that, sweetheart?" Mother said knowingly, dumping the carrots and potatoes into the pot.

"The *story,*" Bobby pleaded, his little legs pumping up and down like there was no tomorrow.

"I have to finish making dinner, dear. Maybe if you asked your sister nicely she'd tell you."

Debbie felt a strong little grip on her arm, pulling her away from the stove. Laughing, not resisting, she said, "Do you want something, shorty?"

"Tell me the story, puhleeze!"

"What story is that?" Debbie asked innocently.

Bobby began howling.

"Okay, okay," she said, sitting down at the kitchen table, Bobby climbing onto her knee. "Now, correct me if I'm wrong, but you want to hear the story of the Easter Bunny, right?"

"No, no, not the *Easter Bunny!*" protested Bobby.

"The Pilgrims?"

"No!"

"Don't tease him, Debra," Mother said.

"Santa Claus?"

"Not *Santy* Claus!" Bobby desperately corrected her. "*Anti* Claus!*"

"Okay, kid, hang on, here we go," Debbie began, her brother settling in with relief, listening to her with wide eyes. "Now, even as we speak the Anti Claus is in his secret workshop, busy sharpening his knives and cleaning his guns, getting ready for the big night. He's making a list and checking it twice. Oh, you'd better watch out, because Anti Claus is coming to town! Nothing will stop him from making his trip on Serial Killer Eve. Not rain, not sleet, and not the police. We'll all be snug in our beds, with visions of mayhem dancing in our heads. In the middle of the night he'll come through the window, making such a clatter, and some poor soul will get up and there will be *such* a splatter. But every home won't get a visit from the Anti Claus, just one, one a year. The Anti Claus has been making his annual visit for over twenty years now and he hasn't forgotten us yet."

"Will he bring presents?"

"The presents the Anti Claus brings you don't want to get."

"Can we paint our house so he doesn't come here?" Bobby asked.

"No, that wouldn't be fair," explained Debbie. "The Gears lost one daughter, and he won't come for their other one if they put the *x*'s on their doors and windows. Nobody knows why. He respects it for some reason, or maybe he doesn't want to get into a rut for goodness sake."

"You shouldn't worry about him coming to our house, Bobby," Mother said. "There are four thousand three hundred seventeen people in Standard Springs, not including the migrant workers. Think of how many people that is! Remember your piggy bank? How many pennies were in there?"

"Three hundred and eighty-one!"

"So if you took ten or eleven piggy banks like that and broke them, and put all the pennies in a big pile and then picked just one penny out of all those pennies, then that would be the chances of him getting you."

"That's a lot of pennies!" Bobby agreed.

"Yes, buster," said Debbie. "We'll look out for you. You can sleep in my room if you want."

"Does the Anti Claus have reindeer?" asked the kid.

"No," said his mother, "I believe one foggy Serial Killer Eve a few years ago the authorities spotted a black Chevy speeding out of town, the red taillights giving off a glow so bright in the fog. But they weren't close enough to see the license plate, so it may have just been some hot-rodding high schooler."

"Can I go on rides this year?" Bobby said.

"We'll have to talk it over with your father."

"He could go with Roger and me," said Debbie. "I'm sure Rog wouldn't mind. I'll call and ask him if it's okay. You like Roger, don't you, Bobby?"

"Sure!"

"See, Mother? Bobby can go with me. Dad won't mind. I mean, he practically invented Serial Killer Days."

"He's just in charge of the parade." Her mother swept a pile of diced onions from the cutting board into the pot, plopped the cover on, and nudged down the heat. "And that's plenty, mind you. Seems like all we see of him after Groundhog Day is the back of his head going out the door. He's even too busy to be afraid."

Debbie helped clean up, dumping the potato eyes and carrot heads into the garbage, then went up to her bedroom, the months of anticipation about this year's pageant narrowing into a tunnel of concentration. She worked on her gown for a while, adding a few more shimmering black sequins down the left sleeve, then lay on her stomach on the foot of the bed and read Rimbaud, the warm summer wind gently pushing back the curtains as his forlorn words stirred her soul.

The phone rang, and after a moment her mother called up, "Debbie Sue, it's Roger!"

Debbie stretched back to grab the phone from the nightstand.

"I've got it, Mom," Debbie said, and when she heard the clunk as her mother hung up the receiver, she said, "Hi, boo boy."

"How's my Queen today?"

"Just grand. What are you doing?"

"Practicin' my lines for the musical. Do you think someone who's hit with a blunt object would shriek or grunt?"

"If it was me I would grunt." Her voice got sad. "I'm not much of a shrieker, I guess. That's what I'm told, anyway."

"What are you talkin' about? Who told you that?"

"Mrs. Toddler. She likes Molly Lovey better than me."

"She's a crazy old bat," Roger said. "You're the best screamer around. You've got real style, baby. Don't talk to me about no Molly Lovey. She's nowhere. She's just got a big act goin' for herself. You're gonna beat her this year."

"Gosh, Rog, the way you say it I almost believe you."

"Believe it. Hey, you need to get your mind off this stuff. The gang's goin' to the drive-in tonight. Big double feature, *Terror Fridge* and *Home on Deranged.* Wanna go?"

"Who's in that last one?"

"Why, none other than Gunnar Graw," said Roger. "He plays a cowboy whose horse expires so he goes nuts and starts stalkin' the local school marm."

"Okay. What time do you want to pick me up?"

"The show starts at dusk, baby."

"I'll be ready. See you later."

"I'll be there so you be there."

"Okay, *good-bye,*" Debbie said with finality.

"I'll pick you up, then."

"Great!"

"I'll be there."

"Do you want me to drive, Rog?"

"You're gonna have to, baby. My wheels aren't in a mobile state. I think I cracked an axle last weekend when I jumped the drainage ditch over by Shaky Bridge."

"I'll be by around eight then. Don't eat anything before I get there."

Her spirits buoyed by Roger's confidence in her, Debbie spent the afternoon reciting Rimbaud and staring at her face in the mirror, trying to instill fear in her countenance. But no matter how much she prodded and poked it, there seemed to be no getting rid of that darn cheerful expression. She tried thinking all sorts of terrible things, oh, like getting gum stuck in her hair or drinking a glass of orange juice gone bad, but her natural good-naturedness would not retreat. Why can't I pretend like Molly? she wondered. Just for that hour when I'm on stage. *Just for an hour.* Why can't I even do that?

I can't blame my folks, Debbie said to herself. I know they did everything they could to bring me up right. For goodness sake, we've been going to Serial Killer Days as long as I can remember. Bobby's plenty scared; he may not be old enough to know exactly what's going on, but I think he realizes that something just awful is going to happen next week.

A bird screeched outside, sending Debbie to the window, her fleeting moment of reflection vaporizing as abruptly as it had formed.

She waved and smiled at Mr. Grackle, rocking back and forth on the telephone wire. You're looking well today, sir, she thought. The bird screeched again.

You're welcome.

●

The family had their first spoonful of soup poised at their lips, having waited the mandatory half hour, when Father came bursting in the house. He unfurled a set of blueprints across the table, his usual look of desperation in his eyes.

"June, kids, lo-lo-look at this," he stammered, nervously running a trembling hand through his thinning blond hair. He was supposed to be on vacation—he always took time off from the real estate office the week before the parade—but he sure doesn't appear to be enjoying himself, Debbie thought, removing a corner of the plans that had dipped into her soup bowl.

"We had two more new entries today," he said with exasperation, "from Burgerama and the Atlantis County Mosquito Control District, both major units. I don't know where to put them. I left a gap between the Paristown High Band and the Shriners, but there isn't room for both of them. One maybe, but not both. Not both!"

"Can't they just squeeze together?" asked his bride.

"No! It's going to require a massive rearrangement! The marshaling and dispersal areas will have to be totally reworked! The whole coordination of the parade may be compromised!"

"Can't you just put them at the end of the line?" Mrs. Morning asked. "After all, they were late."

"No, no, no!" he said impatiently. "You don't understand. Every parade has its own rhythm, every parade has its own story. You build emotion, expectations, you give the audience something and you take it away. The rules that govern a parade are as strict as the rules that control the sun and the moon and the planets. You can't put Burgerama and the Mosquito Control District willy-nilly at the end of the parade. It's simply not done! I'd be laughed out of town!"

"Well, I'm sure you'll think of something," Mother said, reassuringly patting his arm.

He looked at her with anguish, his slightly chubby face creased and pale. "But what if I can't? What if it gets all fouled up? *What if no one can move anywhere?*" He began weeping.

"Why don't you have some soup? I put a ham hock in it."

"Don't have time for a nap now," he said softly, composing himself. He folded up the blueprints and gave his wife a peck on the cheek. "The soup was wonderful. You should make it more often." He stroked Bobby's scalp. "Don't forget to do your homework, boy."

"But it's summer!" Bobby whined.

"Dad, could you stop down at the lumber yard tomorrow and help us with the float?" Debbie asked. "We're having some major festoon problems."

"Ah yes, the festoon," Father said, nodding sagely. "What time will you be down there?"

"Probably by nine or so."

"I'll make it my first stop." Tucking the plans under his arm, he waved a salute at the family unit and turned smartly on his heel, heading for the egress.

"When will you be back?" Mother called after him.

"Twenty-one hundred hours, I suspect. If I'm later, don't wait up for me!"

And they sat and watched the back of his head go out the door.

"I wish he would take it easy once in a while," Debbie worried. "I'm afraid he's going to get an ulcer."

"Remind me to save the recipe for the soup," said her mother.

●

Around eight Debbie grabbed her purse and a fuzzy green blanket and went to the garage. Lifting the door, she gazed with resignation at the bright red vehicle tucked in the corner by the nail barrel. Okay, so it wasn't a sleek white convertible like Molly Lovey drove. Okay, so it wasn't even exactly a normal car. But it had four wheels and it could get you from here to there and it was way better than walking. And Dad got a good price on it to boot.

Hunching down, Debbie opened the driver's door, jammed the blanket under the seat, and stuck her right leg into the car, tucking her knee under the steering wheel. Then she lowered her head and tried to slip it in.

"Oww!" she exclaimed, bumping her noggin on the door frame.

She tried again, more carefully this time, and breathed a deep breath when she was successful. Now for the left leg. She made a couple attempts to slide it in, then grabbed the leg above the knee with both hands and gave it a yank. There. Finally, she reached over with her pinky and pulled the door shut.

How the heck do clowns make it look so easy? Debbie wondered.

The diminutive car started up easily, and she zipped out of the garage, down the driveway, and up the street to Roger's house, which was next door to Molly Lovey's place. She gave a toot on the horn, sounding like a big red squeeze nose. Roger came bounding down the steps a moment later.

Fortunately, her boyfriend was only slightly taller than she, and there wasn't an obstruction like a steering wheel on his side, so it took him just a couple of minutes to wedge himself into the car.

"You want me to drive?" Roger asked with a wicked grin.

"No, it's okay," she said in a melancholy tone.

"You look a little glummed out, baby," said Roger, squirming to get comfortable. "What's the matter?"

She shrugged with her eyes, there not being enough room to shrug with anything else.

"What is it, baby? You can tell me."

"I . . . I just don't feel afraid," she finally said. "Why do you go out with me? There are plenty of girls around more afraid than I am."

"Look," he said, "fear isn't everything, you know. If that's all I wanted I could go out with Molly Lovey or somebody."

"You like her, don't you?"

"Well, I don't know, yeah, I guess I do some. But I don't think I could take the screamin'. I've been hearin' her cries in the middle of the night. That's all she ever thinks about, winnin' that dang contest."

"She practices in the middle of the night?"

"Yeah, she woke me up just last night with her screechin'. It doesn't last long. If it did, I'd call the cops on her. Heh-heh, that would be a riot, seein' Molly hauled away in cuffs."

Gosh, Debbie thought, I didn't realize she was so dedicated. Or maybe it isn't dedication, just her own darn selfishness. I know Mom and Dad wouldn't let me practice my screaming in the middle of the night; I'd get grounded for a month. Her parents bought that nice car for her and seem to let her come and go as she pleases, so they probably don't care if she howls like a dog at 3:00 A.M. either.

"I can't beat her, can I, Rog?"

" 'Course you can. Nobody's unbeatable. You've got the fear in you, I know you do." He took her hand. "I'd do anything to help you win, baby. Anything. I'll prove to you that I'm your dark angel."

Debbie's heart quickened. She had been fanning hopes for weeks that this would be the summer when Roger would bring up the *m* word, and she didn't mean mayhem. He said nothing more now, so she kept driving, quiet and hopeful.

They had left plenty early, and it was just turning dusky as they puttered down the long gravel road leading to the Dark Sky Drive-In on the outskirts of town. It was pretty crowded, teens from all over Atlantis County had made it a favorite hangout, but Debbie figured it wouldn't be too tough finding a spot for their pint-size car.

"Pull up real close, baby," said Roger. "I don't want no four-by-four blockin' my view of Gunnar Graw when he goes nuts."

She parked a couple rows from the front, getting a good running start in order to make it to the top of the hillock. They extracted themselves from the auto and spread out the blanket in front of the car. Roger unclipped the speaker from the stand and hooked it onto the grille of the clown car. Mosquitoes buzzed their heads, but a breeze seemed to be kicking up from the south.

The massive screen was still dark, so they wandered through the lot hand in hand, Roger shooting smart comments at familiar faces, Debbie just smiling at friends she saw along the way.

"I'm gonna get me a Spunky Cola," Roger said as they neared the main building, all decorated with blinking black lights and bunting. "You want anything?"

"I'd have a cola, too," Debbie said. "But I have to use the bathroom first. I'll meet you out front."

"Sure thing, sweets."

Debbie went inside and headed for the ladies' room. As she pushed open the door, she caught a quick glimpse of a person standing at the sink, someone she would rather not run into. It was Molly Lovey. Debbie let the door swing shut without stepping inside. This is silly, she thought, standing there. I have as much right to use that bathroom as she does. Am I going to let her intimidate me just because we're not exactly best friends?

Her decision-making process was rendered moot a second later as the door whipped open from the other side, thunking against Debbie's knee. She let out a yelp and stumbled backward.

"Golly, Deb, are you all right?" Molly Lovey asked, taking Debbie's arm. "I didn't mean to hurt you. I didn't know anyone was standing there."

"No, don't worry, I'm okay," Debbie said, not looking at her. Molly was always so poised, always knew the right things to say in awkward situations like this.

"Boy, that sure was clumsy of me. If I act like that next week I'll be out of luck, don't you think?"

Now Debbie turned her head toward her rival. Molly was grinning. Debbie forced a wan smile in return. "So I hear you've been practicing your screaming in the middle of the night," she said. "You must really want to be Queen again."

"In the middle of the night?" the Queen said oddly. "Who on earth told you that? Well, it doesn't matter because whoever told you that is just making up stories. I'm dead out by ten o'clock most nights." She giggled self-consciously. "Except for the weekends, of course. Do you like Gunnar Graw?"

"He's okay, I guess. Roger thinks he's really cool."

"I think he's cute, although I understand in this picture he sort of acts inappropriately. But he'll probably even be a cute loony tune."

Debbie nodded noncommittally. "I don't mean to cut this short, but I've got to go to the bathroom pretty bad."

"I'll see you in the morning, then," said Molly. "We've got a lot of work left on the float. It was nine o'clock, right?"

"Yes," said Debbie. "Oh, my dad is going to stop in and give us tips on the festoon."

"That would be great. He's always so helpful. See you later."

Debbie watched Molly leave, then she went into the bathroom. As she sat on the toilet, Debbie turned over her suspicions in her mind. Traditionally, Scream Queen contestants acted nicer toward each other as the hours counting down to the pageant dwindled away. They had to, if for no other reason than they were required to perform together on pageant night and work together on the Scream Queen float. Most of it was phony; they would go on being jealous and snotty toward each other once the festivities had ended.

But she wondered if there was something more to Molly's pleasant demeanor. Maybe she was being nice to me because she's afraid she's going to lose this year. Maybe she thinks I won't try as hard if she pretends we're pals. Or maybe, Debbie thought, she strained her voice practicing and would only be able to muster a hoarse bleat come pageant night. But her speaking voice sounded fine.

Not knowing what to think, Debbie flushed, and soon she met Roger as he was carrying the drinks out the door.

"Here, let me take one," she said. They headed back toward the car as a public service cartoon played on the screen. A cartoon teenager at a drive-in threw a pop can out his window. A cartoon cop raced over and beat the litterer to a bloody pulp. Hoots and car honks filled the air. An admonition flashed strobe-like on the big screen: FOR YOUR SAKE, PLEASE DON'T BE A LITTER BUG.

"I ran into Molly coming out of the bathroom," said Debbie, taking a long draw on the straw. "We started talking and she starts saying she never practices her screaming in the middle of the night."

"Oh, she's just a big liar," Roger said. "It was her, all right, and I had the headache to prove it. It's strategy, don't you see? She's tryin' to psych you out, get you off guard."

"That's sort of what I was thinking. I'm wondering if maybe there isn't something wrong with her voice."

"Could be, baby, could be."

The honking grew to a crescendo, and the movie began.

Debbie didn't care for the film, although Roger seemed to be enjoying himself. It was nice to lie beside him on the blanket, anyway. She tried to scrape together her courage and bring up the marriage question, telling herself that it was a natural thing. After all, they had talked about it over the winter, in a general, skittish way, and she assumed they would get hitched soon; he would take over his father's feed store, she would bear as many children as technically feasible, and they would live in Standard Springs forever.

But just as she was about to speak her heart, Gunnar Graw attacked the school marm with a hacksaw, severing an artery in her arm which sent a 150-foot stream of blood spraying across the screen.

"You know, baby," Roger said, putting his arm around Debbie, "it's a darn shame that Serial Killer Days only comes but once a year."

3

Lamprey's Lumber Yard was a source of some tension for Arvid Morning. Years ago when he was in high school, a windstorm hit the yard, scattering the neat, perfectly ordered rows of one-by-nines and six-by-threes. A disturbing sight for any normal person. Arvid avoided the area for days afterward, until he had heard from a friend that the lumber had been straightened up.

Now, even some thirty years later, an involuntary shudder came over Arvid as he parked his car outside the sea green corrugated building, where a cluster of bicycles were propped up.

Don Lamprey greeted him as he stepped inside, the air and Lamprey's slick red hair hazy from the sawdust. In the far corner a coterie of young women stood around the frame of a float.

"Mornin', Arv," said the owner. "How's the parade looking?"

"A few snags here and there, but nothing we can't handle." Arvid took this tact to keep morale high. Actually, he had been up most of the night reworking the master plan, and had somehow managed to fit the two new units in without disturbing the headquarters division, the first division which featured the best and brightest units. It was important to make as much of an impact with the head of the parade as possible. Selecting units for the headquarters division was straightforward; it was usually easy to spot the best bands, the most beautiful floats, and so on. But it was another trick altogether to sustain that momentum throughout the course of the parade. As a wag once said, the units in the headquarters division should serve as appetizers for what should be a tasty first course and generally a good dinner.

"We appreciate your willingness to allow the Queen contestants to use your space," said Arvid. "Their float is the most important in the entire parade. It's a grand civic gesture you've made."

"Well, it is a burden, but anything for the ol' community interest, eh?" the lumber man said.

Arvid headed over to the float. When his daughter spotted him, she waved and said, "Hi, Father! How do you like it?"

Circling the float, he nodded, saying, "You girls are doing fine. You're going to need a brace for the apron here. And over here, the lower cross member needs to be elevated so there's enough clearance for the trailer tongue. You said you were having a festoon problem?"

"Yes," said Tabby Sorensen, a tall sophomore with curly black hair. She came over and, kneeling, pointed out the frizzy green cord. "See where the tie points are? Is there anything we can do so it doesn't look so shabby?"

"Hmm," he said, pondering, then replied, "I would suggest rosettes. Do you have any other color festoon? Gold or white would be fine, but avoid red because then it would look like a Christmas float. We'll need scissors, too."

"We've got gold," said Debbie, and brought the items over. The other girls gathered around her dad.

"Now, what you do is cut about a nine-inch length of festoon." He did this, then rolled it into a ball, and placed the ball over the knot in the cord. "Next you loop your tie knot over it and the ball, like so." He cut off the loose ends of cord. "And that's all there is to it."

"Wow, that's neat!" exclaimed Tabby.

"Yeah, Dad, that's great," his daughter said proudly.

"The secret of all good float decoration," Arvid told them in a professorial tone, "is turning apparent liabilities into assets. Float design is a crude, quick art form, and if you're not careful you'll be sitting there on parade day in front of the whole county with your festoons hanging out. So this way, instead of people over-looking this section of the float or even making rude comments about your tie points, they will remark, 'My, what lovely festoon balls!' "

As Arvid completed his inspection of the float, surveying the rear of the unit, he frowned in dismay. A big placard had been inexpertly tacked onto the back frame, beneath the cage: DON'T BE BOARD, SHOP AT LAMPREY'S LUMBER YARD. Shaking his head, Arvid unfastened the sign and said, "Looks good, kids. I'll be right back."

He found the owner in his office, eating a glazed donut. Hold-ing up the illicit placard, Arvid said, "Nice ad, Lamprey."

"Thanks. It took me the better part of a weekend to dream up that jingle. I even wrote a song to go with it. Do you want to hear it? *Oh, if your house needs a fixin' and you don't want to go afar . . .*"

"You know better than that," Arvid interrupted.

"Is something wrong?" asked the man innocently.

"We can't have commercials on the Queen float. It's the focus of the whole parade. You're already listed as a sponsor of the float in the program."

"But I tried to make it as inconspicuous as I could. Heck, Arv, with all those pretty girls, who's going to notice my little ol' sign? I thought as long as I donated the space . . ."

"Well, we appreciate that, Don, believe me, but there can be no compromise when it comes to the sanctity of the Scream Queen."

He handed the sign back to the lumber man, who took it cheer-fully. Returning to the float, Arvid told the contestants, "Let me know if Mr. Lumber tries anything like that again." He looked at them quizzically. "Aren't we missing a Queen here? Who's tardy?"

"That would be her highness," Samantha Sink, last year's third-place finisher, said with a laugh. The whole group snickered.

"I saw Molly at the drive-in last night," Debbie offered. "She said she'd be here at nine."

"Please, please, do not follow in her footsteps," he warned them. "If this was April instead of a week before the parade, then

I wouldn't worry. But these final days are crucial to the success of this enterprise. Those of you who have participated before know what I'm talking about. Two years ago the Scream Queens were scurrying about in the marshaling area as the parade began, trying to attach tissue fringe between the apron frame and the ground to hide the wheels. They had not done a final inspection the day before because they said they were too afraid, but I hardly think that is an adequate excuse." He could feel the flop sweat forming on the back of his neck, as he recalled the jam up it caused. His left eyelid began twitching. He inhaled deeply. "Someone needs to go get her, wake her up or whatever is necessary. Debbie, I'd like you to volunteer."

She winced, but said, "Okay, Dad. I'm on my way." She hurried for the door.

Now he addressed the remaining Queens. "If you need me for anything today, please call me at home. I've got meetings all day and into the evening, but I'll be checking back at home every hour or so for messages."

"Thanks, Mr. Morning," said Tabby. "We're going to make our float the best one in the whole darn parade! Right, girls?"

"RIIIIIGHT!!!"

●

"Thank you all for coming on this lovely Saturday morning," Arvid told the assembled chairmen and chairwomen of the annual Serial Killer Days' Parade of Fear, all seated around a table in his office. "Hopefully, the weather will take a turn for the worse by next week. Yes, I know it's hard to believe that all these months of work will come to a head in a week's time, but it's true. I don't need to remind any of you of the vigilance required in these last few, precious days. I just visited the Scream Queen's float and those young women are all doing a fine job; they're all working so hard and I know they'll make us proud. Now, let's start with the committee updates. Why don't we begin with the treasury committee?"

"Thank you, Arv," said Franklin Wrisky Jr., co-executive sub-officer at Wrisky Savings and Loan. "If my figures are correct—and I work in a bank so they'd better be!—but if my figures are right I'm showing us two hundred forty-nine dollars in the black as of this morning. This is due in large part to the fine turnout at last weekend's blood drive. However, this does not take into account the high school bands from Golbyville and Nodal, both of which are holding out for more money."

"How serious are they?" asked the chairman. "Are they playing us off another town's parade? Do you think they have another offer?"

"Hard to say. It's that old 'making high school kids march in the middle of the night' business again, the little whiners. We're already offering them twenty percent more than any other parade in the county."

Shaking his head, Arvid said, "If it was some smaller unit in the rear of the parade, then I would say let's squeeze them a bit, but the Golbyville band is in the headquarters division, and we can't afford to lose them. They're the only band that brings their own weapons. Offer them another hundred bucks and see if Burgerama will give them some fries for the ride home."

"What about Nodal?"

"Let them sweat it out."

"Right, chief."

"Now," Arvid said, making a notation in his official parade notebook, "why don't we hear from the Souvenir Committee? Mary Beth Jo?"

"Thanks, Arv," said Mary Beth Jo Raisin, co-owner of Raisin Implement. "I'm happy to report that the storefront souvenir shop, which we opened this past week—next to Smell's Shoe Store if you want to stop in—has been doing great business. The buttons and caps and T-shirts are selling as fast as they always have, and I am pleased to announce that the Official Serial Killer Days' Snow Globe, which we introduced this year, is selling very well. I brought one along if you haven't seen it yet." She reached into a bag and removed a little plastic globe filled with dark red-colored liquid and a tableau depicting a somewhat generic-looking small town main street with a tiny Serial Killer Days' banner strung across it. She tipped the globe upside down and shook it. Black snowflakes whipped through the town for a few seconds before settling gently on the bottom of the globe. "See how pretty?" she said.

"Very nice job, Mary Beth Jo," Arvid said. "The kids will love it." He shuffled his papers, then said, "Let's see, next up, Law and Order Committee. Deputy Dan?"

"Yes, uh, thank you, Mr. Morning, friends and colleagues," said the officer in a quiet voice, tugging at the collar of his neatly pressed shirt. His eyes remained riveted to the yellow legal pad he was holding, which trembled slightly as he spoke. "The Law and Order Committee reports that the parking situation is *completely* under control. The city lot on Main and Fourth Street has been *completely* repaved and I am scheduled to hose down the traffic cones this morning. Signs designating auxiliary parking areas at the middle school and Slippery Park will be removed from the closet by myself and *completely* inspected."

"Any problems getting volunteer help for parade day?"

"That situation is under control. We will again be using local cub scouts and brownies. Twenty-two have signed up so far down at the station, which is one less than last year, two less than the year before. I have no information on the reason for the decline of volunteerism in our community."

"I wouldn't worry about it. Anything else to report?"

"No, Mr. Morning."

"Thank you, then."

The Deputy self-consciously rose and left the room.

"While we're on the subject," the chairman continued, "any update on the, uh, special guest situation, Judge Flail?"

"Nothing yet," said the Judge, a white-haired man with a bulbous red nose. "We're working on it, though. I talked to Warden Junker at PowPow Penitentiary last night. To be frank about it, he said to stop calling him because there is no way in hell he is going to release a murderer or a child molester or even a jaywalker to be put on display in some hick town parade. Those are his words, by the way. He sounded like he had his mind made up. Maybe I caught him on a bad day."

"Who do we have locked up in town?"

"Slim pickings, I'm afraid. Bad checks, DWIs, domestic abuse."

"Do they *look* dangerous?"

"The DWI looks pretty bad. I could knock off a month from his sentence if he'll ride the float. . . ."

"Sure, that would be fine. Let me know if anyone else comes in this week, though."

"Right."

"By the way, how is *your* float coming along?"

"Just fine," said the Judge, "although I am having a helluva time with the tinsel flitter. . . ."

•

Originally scheduled for the second Thursday every month, the Standard Springs City Council meeting for July was moved up to the Saturday afternoon before the start of Serial Killer Days. Most of the elected officials held vital roles in seeing that the festivities went off without a hitch, from Sven Lagoon, who played the lead role in the musical, to Dottie East, a retired history teacher who was one of the group of volunteers that led educational tours to the sites of the most notable Serial Killer Eve attacks. Had Debbie volunteered again? Arvid wondered, realizing with paternal shame that he hadn't spoken with his daughter in days.

The council meeting was traditionally a casual, devil-may-care affair, with glad tidings of great fear in every heart.

Arvid took his usual spot in the front row, seeing that the meeting room in back of the Princess Theater was otherwise devoid of spectators apart from local newspaperman Griff Grimes, who was slouched in the back row, peeling an apple with a paring knife.

The council members recited the Pledge of Allegiance and the Lord's Prayer, and the Mayor, Dr. Sellit, threw in the Hippocratic oath for good measure.

"Arvid, I know you're busy, so why don't we take care of your business first so you can get back to work."

"Thank you, Mayor. I appreciate it."

Councilman Gender, a construction contractor known for his sense of humor, poked his white-socked toes under the apron at the bottom of the table and wiggled them at Dottie East, who stifled a laugh and looked away.

"Now, what I gathered from the agenda item you submitted," said the Mayor, thumbing through a stack of papers, the other members doing the same, "is that you want the council to consider changing the name of our town from Standard Springs to Serial Killer, is that right?"

"Yes, Mayor."

"Here it is," he said, pulling a single sheet out of the pile. He read it silently for a minute, then said, "I don't see it on here, but I assume you mean the name change to be in force only during the week of the festival, correct?"

"No, Mayor," Arvid replied. "What I have in mind is a permanent change. It's what we're identified with anyway. Why not capitalize on it all the way?"

"Serial Killer, Minnesota," the Mayor said quietly. "I don't know, Arv. What does everyone else think?"

"I think we've gone pretty far in this area already," said Gender, toes hidden again. "Heck, we've already got Bludgeon Street and Pain Lane."

"I've got a reputation as being someone who's pretty tight with a buck when it comes to spending the taxpayers' money," worried the Mayor. "I'm trying to think of the expense involved in adopting a new name. We'd have to change the stationery, repaint the water tower . . ." He turned to the city manager. "Lucas, what do you think about this?"

"Actually," the city manager said, "the water tower is going to need repainting some time next year anyway. I want to hear what Arvid has in mind before we go any further."

"I'm not some naive dreamer," said Arvid, standing up. "I'm

suggesting this change for very practical reasons. We would become a Mecca for those attracted to the macabre, and guarantee ourselves a steady annual tourist flow, not just a huge influx one week of the year. The way I see it, we've got this small problem: Some fellow comes to our town once a year and kills somebody. What town doesn't have problems? Okay, we've taken advantage of it up to a point, and we're pretty pleased with ourselves, but check around the country and see how many people have even heard of Standard Springs or know where it is. Forgive me for using a cliché, but changing our name to Serial Killer would put our town on the map."

There was a contemplative silence for a few moments before Lucas said, "I've heard rumors that the Beethead family is talking about shutting down the sausage plant next year. The city would take a huge tax hit if it happened. Combine that fact with the exodus of our young people and the drying up of federal and state dollars and I don't believe we should reject an option like this out of hand."

"Not to mention the Big Big Store," said the Mayor, referring to the discount warehouse store out on the highway, which had a groundbreaking ceremony last week. "Once they come in, Main Street is going to be hurting."

"I'm not sure I like the idea," said Dottie.

"We could finally build that water slide," Gender said wistfully.

"Well, we're not going to decide anything today," the Mayor told them. "Let's put the matter on the agenda again next month, and in the meantime I want Lucas to do some research and the rest of you ask around town and see what people think. I imagine it would have to be put up to a referendum. I certainly wouldn't want to leave a decision like this to the six of us. If the voters go for it and it fails miserably, they'll have nobody to blame but themselves."

There were murmurs of agreement.

"Actually," Lucas drawled, "with all due respect, Mr. Mayor, I'm not sure you're entirely correct."

"I'm not?" the Mayor said.

"I may be off the mark here," said Lucas, "but I believe the city charter leaves such important matters in the hands of the town's duly elected representatives. . . ."

4

That rotten old Molly Lovey!

Debbie corralled her bicycle from where she had left it beside the front door of Lamprey's Lumber Yard. Sneezing, she thought: Great, she goofs off and I'm the one who has to track her down. Before Debbie left she had tried calling the Queen, but the phone rang and rang and rang. Knowing her, she was probably still dead asleep.

So I'll start at her house and save us all some time, Debbie decided, pedaling her bike onto Fall Street. When she got to Bludgeon, she hung a right and headed up the avenue to the ivy-choked house. As the pinkish dwelling came into view, she spotted Roger's scruffy sneakers poking out from underneath an old green sedan next door. Pulling into his driveway, she rolled quietly up to him and bumped her tire against the sole of his shoe.

"Hey, what?" a muffled voice said, the boy wriggling out from under the heap.

"Hey, you!" said Debbie, grinning, leaning out over her handlebars. "Whatcha doing?"

Roger broke into smiling, his face streaked with grease. "Bye-bye clown car!" he announced proudly. "The damage ain't as bad as I thought. I'll have my baby on the road by the end of the weekend."

"Great!"

"You're up and around early. I thought you were supposed to be workin' on your float this morning."

"I was," she replied, with a bit of disgust. "But Miss Perfect decided she had something better to do and I got appointed to the search party detail. I figured she just slept in. Have you seen her?"

"You mean Molly?"

"None other."

Sitting up, Rog said, "No, I haven't seen her this morning. She was screamin' again last night, though. Real loud. Practicin', I guess."

"Practicing," Debbie repeated. She thought for a moment, then swiveled her bike around and pushed off. "Call you later!" she yelled back with a wave.

Debbie hopped off her bicycle in the Loveys' front yard, went up and rang the doorbell. There was no answer, so she went around to the back door and got the same result.

Now where? she wondered. Maybe she went to school, or stopped uptown for some reason. Yes, that's it. She's probably gabbing with Annabel Weed down at Weed's Bakery. Pleased with her ability to play detective, Debbie hopped on her bike and headed uptown.

Main Street was just waking up. Mrs. Hamp was sweeping the sidewalk in front of her hardware store, and there was Mr. Grimes, leaving the newspaper office. He knew everyone in town. Maybe he had seen Molly. She squeezed the brake lever and came to a halt just outside the Standard Springs Herald.

"Morning, Mr. Grimes."

The editor, a dark-eyed man with slick black hair and a week's worth of stubble, made a gun with his finger and pretended to fire a shot at her. "Hiya, kid. You need to stop in for a snapshot before Monday, maybe a smart quote or two. You're my odds-on favorite for Scream Queen now that it looks like Molly Lovey is out of the picture."

"Out of the picture? What are you talking about?"

"Haven't you heard? They took her to the hospital last night. Some type of seizure, from what I understand."

"My gosh!" exclaimed Debbie. "I've been looking for her. She was supposed to help us work on the float this morning. We thought she was just goofing off. . . ."

"Want to ride along? I'm on my way to the hospital now."

"Yes!"

On the trip to Standard Springs Memorial Hospital, which was located on the east edge of town by the armory, Debbie rode silently, too wrapped up in her own thoughts to say anything. She couldn't believe it. Molly had appeared to be perfectly normal at the drive-in. And now, whammo! She'd have to call the lumber yard and tell her father when she got to the hospital. She felt afraid of how Dad would take the news; Molly played such an integral role in the parade.

They arrived at the hospital and Debbie followed Griff Grimes up the walk to the main entrance.

"Morning, Winnie," he greeted the receptionist. "I'm here on the Molly Lovey case. Where did you stash her?"

"She's in room three thirty-five, but she's not conscious yet. Her parents are up there, though."

"Good enough." Glancing back, he said, "Come on, Debaroo. I need a set of sympathetic eyes."

They rode the elevator to the third floor and headed down the hall. "Here it is," Griff said, stopping at the room. The door was ajar. He snuck a glance inside, then stepped back, gesturing to the solarium at the end of the hall. "Her parents are in there. Let's wait for them to come out. Maybe we can grab the doctor, too."

"I should call some people," Debbie said.

"I want to talk to you first, if you don't mind. It'll just take a couple minutes."

"Okay."

They seated themselves on a blue plastic couch in the lounge, a long window behind them overlooking a cornfield, the green stalks rippling in the wind. Grimes removed a notepad from his shirt pocket and flipped it open to a blank page. He scribbled something down, then looked at Debbie and said, "Your colleague and rival has fallen, Miss Morning, a scant week before the Scream Queen Pageant. What are your thoughts at this very difficult time, when your best friend is laying there in a hospital bed in an unknown condition?"

"Well, to be honest, Mr. Grimes, Molly and I really weren't that close. I felt pretty annoyed by her a lot of the time."

"But that's perfectly natural, you know, to feel that way about a competitor."

"Is it? I didn't know that."

"So you're feeling sad, is that right?"

"Well, I suppose I am. This has all happened so suddenly. I mean, I just saw her last night at the drive-in."

"You did? Did you talk? What was the last thing she said to you?"

"Um, boy, you know I don't remember. I ran into her coming out of the bathroom, and we talked for just a minute, because I really had to go."

"And then you said good-bye?"

"Well, sort of, I guess." She looked at the editor hopefully. "Am I done now?"

"Let me get a picture," he said, removing the lens cover on his camera. "Look mournful!" he suggested. There was a blinding flash.

"Am I done now?" she said, blinking her eyes.

"All done."

She got up and sat down next to the phone. First she thumbed through the phone book until she found the number for Lamprey's Lumber Yard. Debbie had the boy who answered page her father. He had already left, so she spoke to Tabby and told her what happened, then she called home and left a message for her dad. As she was hanging up the phone, Griff Grimes said, "Hoo boy, a hat trick."

Debbie stuck close to him as he started back down the hallway to where Molly's parents were standing along with Dr. Frank Stone outside her room.

". . . more tests to be done," the doctor was saying, and then he leaned in toward Mr. and Mrs. Lovey and said something too softly for Debbie to hear. They nodded, tears in their eyes. The doctor touched Mrs. Lovey's arm and broke away, going back down the corridor. Grimes moved in on the parents, while Debbie pursued the doctor.

"Dr. Stone!" she called as softly as she could.

The man turned, and smiled tiredly at her. "Hello, Debbie."

"What happened to Molly? Is she going to be okay?"

"Well, we're not quite certain about that yet. Her folks brought her in last night about three A.M. She was unconscious but breathing. We believe it was a seizure of some type, although we don't know the source. She may be able to shed some light on this when she regains consciousness. She doesn't have any history of blackouts, although my best hunch, and don't quote me on this, is that she experienced a brain murmur."

"Brain murmur. Is that serious?"

"It depends on the individual, and their lifestyle. For some, it's no more harmful than a minor headache. For others . . ." He shook his head ominously.

"When will she come out of it?"

"Hard to say. Her vital signs are all stable. It could be an hour from now or a week from now. Or longer."

"Gosh," said Debbie, "I feel so sorry for her. Is there anything I can do to help her?"

"I'm afraid not. We're just going to have to let it run its course. . . ."

●

"Now if we can figure out a way to bump off the other three," Roger said when Debbie raced back to his house to tell him the news.

"Roger, that's a terrible thing to say," Debbie told him.

"Hey, it was only a joke. But the truth is you're in and you know it. This is what we've been waitin' for. I'll celebrate if you don't want to."

"I'm not celebrating anything and neither should you," Debbie said crossly. "I know Molly and I aren't best friends or anything, but she is in the hospital, for goodness sake. Besides, she'll probably recover in time for the pageant anyway so there's nothing to talk about, all right?"

"Who's the girl who looks like a dream?" Roger sang. *"It's the way she walks, the way she talks, the way she screams . . ."*

"You stop it, Roger Allen Gumpers! Only the Queen gets that song sung to her, and only on the night of the pageant! What's the matter with you? I swear, you can be so uncouth sometimes." She turned away, taking a step down the driveway.

"Aw, I didn't mean nothin'." Touching her shoulder, he said, "I can't help it that I'm happy. You know I want you to win that contest more than anything in the world. You deserve it. It's fate, can't you see?"

Facing him again, she took his hand. "I know you're awfully fond of me, Roger. A girl couldn't ask for a guy more loyal than you. But this is serious. What if she never wakes up? What if she never screams again? I want to walk down that aisle, too; it would be the greatest, but I want to win fair and square, against the best there is. I'd rather lose with her competing than win like this."

"Well, it won't matter because you're gonna win anyway," said Roger, "with or without Molly Lovey."

Traffic *cones.*

On his way back to headquarters from the weekly Serial Killer Days Committee meeting, Deputy Dan spotted Junior Sasser in Victory Park. The Deputy was all hepped up to hose off the cones in preparation for the masses of strangers that would descend on Standard Springs next week, but such official business would have to wait. A retiree from the Dim Line Railway Company, where he had worked as a switchman for forty years, Junior spent his freedom finding ways to keep busy, most innocent enough, a few potentially dangerous. Once he tried to climb to the top of Ol' Oakie, the biggest oak tree in town, in his long johns. Barn door got hooked on a branch halfway up and the fire department had to be called to extract him.

Now he was wandering through the park with a pointed stick. Deputy Dan cut across the baseball diamond and intercepted him.

"Morning, Junior," said the Deputy.

Hands clasped around the ends of a forked stick, Junior kept his eyes on the ground, walking in a slow, zigzagging route through the clover and dandelions.

"I said, Good morning, Junior," the Deputy repeated, skipping to keep out of the man's way.

"I hear ya," Junior said testily. "Can't you see I'm tryin' to concentrate?"

"What are you doing? We've got plenty of wells in the city, you know."

"Ain't lookin' for water."

"What are you looking for, then?"

"Ain't tellin'."

"Junior, you have to tell me. I'm an officer of the law and it's my judgment that you're engaging in suspicious activity."

Junior said nothing for a while, but Deputy Dan stayed right on his tail, and finally the old man said, "It's my brother."

"Okay, Junior, what did you do to your brother?"

"Didn't do nothin' to him. I just can't let it happen again this year. You know, he finds that gosh darn prize every year, and it ain't because he's all that much smarter than me, it's because he's rich enough to send away for all these space-age gizmos, and I've had enough of it. So I've been readin' books about divinin' rods and this year *I'm* the one who's gonna get the big prize."

Grabbing the man's sleeve, Deputy Dan said, "For gosh sake, Junior, the prize hasn't even been buried yet! They don't do that until tomorrow night!"

Junior stopped and appeared to contemplate this development for a moment, then replied, "Well, I'm just tryin' to see where they're *going* to bury it. Figure I'd save myself a little time."

"Those witchin' sticks really work?" Deputy Dan asked, tipping up his cap.

"Oh, sure," said Junior. "You can find water, or a lost ring or oil or pretty much anything. They say when Christopher Columbus got lost he used it to discover America. The human body is an electrical appliance, you know. Here, why don't you give it a try?" He offered Dan the stick.

The Deputy took it, inspecting it carefully. Clasping both ends of the fork, he pointed it at the ground.

"Don't point it," said Junior. "It'll point you."

"I don't feel anything."

"Well, what are you lookin' for?"

Shaking his head, the Deputy handed it back to him. "I think

I'll stick to my standard law enforcement equipment, Junior. Hope you find something with it, though."

"I can feel the vibrations already," said Junior, his wrinkled fingers trembling.

As he headed back to the jailhouse, Deputy Dan felt a little ashamed that he didn't know more about the divining stick. Junior is my intellectual superior, Deputy Dan thought glumly. But he gets to sit around at the library all day and read odd books while I vowed to keep the streets of Standard Springs, and its outlying areas, safe and secure. I can tell you about Mrs. Zipple's cat Abby who keeps getting stuck in her chimney or what kind of pop bottles kids are throwing at street lamps nowadays, but anything beyond the county line and into the realm of divining rods or space-age gizmos and I'm a hopeless case.

As he crossed the street in front of Raisin Implement, Dan contemplated the possibility of employing the divining stick in his silent crusade to track down the serial killer. A man like that must send off some *mighty serious vibrations*. But how long do the vibrations stay fresh? If the answer was a long time, then he was sunk because over the years the killer had probably set foot on every street in town.

But if the stick only picked up the vibrations of the living thing . . .

It would be perfect. He could use it next week to test out his theory, that the serial killer actually took part in the parade every year. Most parades are crashed by individuals who are "parade happy," who show up, usually disguised as clowns or other costumed characters, when the parade begins and march right along. The crowd thinks they are part of the festivities, and, amid the chaos of a typical parade, officials ascribe responsibility for them to someone else in the chain of command. In other years Deputy Dan had tried buttonholing these impostors, but they invariably disappeared quickly into the crowds. It was his theory that the killer used the vantage point of a parade participant—all those faces looking like a fast food menu—to choose that year's victim.

So what were the options? Outlaw all nonhuman parade participants? Or cancel the parade altogether?

Maybe I should ask the Sheriff, he mused, and then thought better of it, deciding to wait until the idea was chewed on enough for someone to digest.

●

When Deputy Dan arrived back at the station, Sheriff Eeha motioned him over to his desk and said, "I've got a real dilemma here."

"A dilemma?" Dan asked, growing excited. "What happened?"

"I'm trying to decide what slogan to put on my campaign signs. What do you think sounds better, Danny: 'Law and Order and a Whole Lot More' or 'I Won't Take Your Gun Unless It's Not Yours?' He sat there, pen poised.

"Uh, I like the first one better."

"Me, too, but I'm still not sure it's a winner. And it's gotta be a winner because it sounds like Rodney Owl is really going to go after us this election. Some of the boys at the Pain Cafe say he's telling people we aren't doing our jobs, that we've got all these unsolved murders on our hands. Shucks, we only get one murder in town a year! That's not too bad a record. What about all the other days of the year when *nobody* gets killed? And it's just one guy; it's not like there's a hoard of maniacs running loose around town. I'll put my record up against any sheriff anywhere."

"We'll catch him one of these years, I know we will."

"But that's not the point! This office does an outstanding job for this town three hundred sixty-five days a year, including on parade day. We can't go on wild goose chases on the busiest night of the year. Who would handle the parking?"

"It'd be a mess," Deputy Dan agreed.

"If we raced around town the night of the parade looking for some nut instead of doing our job, there'd probably be more than one person who'd die. Some kid would get run over in a parking lot or something."

"Boy, I don't even want to think about that."

"Of course these subtleties are overlooked when you got some-one like Rodney Owl going around exaggerating the facts and playing on people's fears," the Sheriff huffed.

"Do you want me to hose down the traffic cones now?" asked Deputy Dan.

"Yes, and make sure to get them nice and shiny," the Sheriff said. "Remember, people from all over Atlantis County are coming here next week and we won't have a second chance to make a good impression."

So Deputy Dan got the cones out of the storage locker and took them back behind the station. After he spread them in a semicircular pattern on the blacktop, he unwound the hose and turned on the water. Too fine a spray! They'll never get shiny that way, he thought. He twisted the nozzle and soon had a nice lusty stream of water pounding against the surface of the cones. He smiled, pleased at how well he had handled this task. Too bad the Sheriff isn't here to see it, he thought.

When he was finished, Deputy Dan hung up the hose and brought the cones inside so they wouldn't get all dusty again. He brought a stack of them into the office, holding them up for Sheriff Eeha to see, but he was on the phone.

"Yes, Mrs. Flatwire, that is a criminal act . . . Wouldn't an apology be enough? . . . Yes, ma'am, I know you pay my salary . . . For gosh sakes, it was only an apple! . . . All right, all right, I'll send someone over right away." The Sheriff hung up the phone, expelling a burst of air.

"Criminal act?" Deputy Dan asked.

"Oh, it's Mrs. Flatwire," said Sheriff Eeha. "Someone's been in her apple trees again. She's got a gun on the guy. Why don't you go out and calm her down and bring the fella in, for his own safety?"

"Right," Dan said, setting down the cones. Boy, he thought, a real criminal act. It's almost a hostage situation.

"Nice work, by the way!" the Sheriff called out as the Deputy grabbed his hat and made for the door.

Deputy Dan turned back, puzzled.

"The cones, boy, the cones! Don't think I didn't notice!"

"Thanks!" said the Deputy, beaming proudly.

He climbed into the squad car and pulled out onto Main, flipping on the siren. A dog ran across the street, cowering. In a short time Deputy Dan arrived at the scene on the south end of town. Mrs. Flatwire lived in an Egyptian-styled Victorian house, a grove of apple trees out back, her prize Jonathans which she entered in the county and state fairs every year. He parked and cut around the house to the orchard.

There they were.

Mrs. Flatwire, perhaps seventy-five, wearing a blue nightgown with tea kettles on it, was holding what appeared to be a .22 rifle on the perpetrator, a lanky, dark-haired man in his forties dressed in patched jeans and a blue work shirt, a small notebook poking out of his shirt pocket. The man was seated on the ground, arms clasped around his knees. His expression was surprisingly placid, looking up at her without fear. An apple with two large chunks eaten out of it lay midway between him and the woman.

"Put the gun down, Mrs. Flatwire," Deputy Dan said, approaching the pair. "We don't want any violence today, do we?"

"It's about time you got here," she said, her gun not wavering. "This is a dangerous criminal. Caught him stealing my apples. 'No trespassing,' says the sign, but he don't pay no attention to it."

Approaching her quickly, the Deputy said, "I'll handle him now, ma'am," and he clasped hold of the rifle's barrel, pointing it harmlessly away, then gently pulled it from her grip. Turning to the captive, he asked, "Where you from?"

"From a far, far friendlier place than this," the man said with a grin.

"Did you see the 'No Trespassing' sign?"

"I thought it said, 'Free Apples.'"

"Why did you take the apple?"

"I was hungry."

"Would you apologize to her?"

"You put him in jail!" Mrs. Flatwire demanded. "I don't want no apology. I'm tired of people thinking they can just walk onto my land any old time they feel like and steal my apples! Next they'll break into my house and hit me over the head and take all my savings from the inside of the piano . . . Oh, shit."

"I'm sorry I picked one of your apples," the man on the ground offered. "It won't happen again. It wasn't that good anyway." He turned up his nose. "Wormy."

"There ain't no worms in my apples!" Mrs. Flatwire shouted. "My apples have won more blue ribbons than you can count!" She reached for her gun, but the Deputy pushed her back. "Let's go," he said to the apple thief. The man slowly rose and led the way back to the house.

"I want my gun back!" said Mrs. Flatwire.

"You can stop down at the station and get it once you settle down."

When they reached the patrol car, the Deputy frisked and handcuffed the apple thief and opened the rear door.

"So what's the deal, am I under arrest?" the man asked, ducking his head as he slid into the backseat.

The Deputy shut the door and got behind the wheel. "Well, that depends on Mrs. Flatwire," said Deputy Dan, laying her rifle on the seat beside him. "We'll give her a couple hours to cool off." He started up the car and pulled away from the house. "She's pretty protective about her apples. I wouldn't worry too much about it, though. Trespassing is just a misdemeanor. Judge Flail will probably let you off with a hundred-buck fine maybe and a written apology."

"A hundred bucks, huh. I didn't even get to finish the apple."

Glancing at the rearview mirror, Deputy Dan said, "Where did you say you were from?"

"I'm what you call a road dog."

"A road dog? You mean you're a bum."

"Aren't words funny?"

"What's your name?"

"If I'm a bum, what darn difference does it make?"

"Have you been in Standard Springs before?"

"Ain't you going to read me my rights?"

"Just making conversation," said the Deputy.

"Well, I have been in Standard Springs before," said the man. "Several times, in fact."

"I don't recollect your face, so you must not have gotten into any trouble here before."

The stranger made no reply and rode silently the rest of the way to the station.

●

"Here's our man," Deputy Dan said, leading the prisoner into the Sheriff's office.

Sheriff Eeha rose and came over, scrutinizing the stranger. "So what's his story?"

"It's like Mrs. Flatwire said. He stole an apple from one of her trees. He was just sitting on the ground when I got there and didn't give me any trouble. But she was so riled up I had to confiscate her rifle."

"Well, take it back to her right away," said the Sheriff. "Did you forget this is an election year?"

"Sorry."

"What's your name?" the Sheriff asked the apple thief.

"Hobo Bob."

"You don't look like no hobo to me."

"I didn't think so either 'til your deputy called me one."

"Do you have any identification?"

"Nope."

"Are you going to tell us your name?"

"Sam Centaur, your honor."

Sheriff Eeha gave the man another long look, then said, "Well, sir, we're going to have to hold onto you for a while. When Mrs. Flatwire cools off we'll see if she still wants to press charges. If she does, you'll be seeing Judge Flail Monday morning. If not, then you're free to go." He patted down the hobo, removing the notebook and a stubby red pencil from his pocket.

"Hey, I need that," said the man.

"You'll get it back when you leave," said the Sheriff, and ushered him into the middle cell.

The Sheriff flipped through the notebook, and shook his head. "That's the worst case of handwriting I have ever seen."

"You keep your nose out of that!" said the stranger hotly.

"Just simmer down. I'm not hurting it." He stuck the notebook into his desk drawer. "If you mind I'll let you have it back later. State says we've got an obligation to rehabilitate our prisoners."

●

When Deputy Dan arrived back at the Flatwire place, he found the victim weeping in the orchard, cradling the damaged apple in her palms like a wounded kitten.

"I'm sorry to disturb you, ma'am, but I brought your gun back."

"Thank you," she said quietly.

"You think you want to press charges against him?"

"I don't know. Do I have to decide now?"

"We can hold him for twenty-four hours. Tomorrow's Sunday, so we'd need to know sometime on Monday."

"Okay, I'll wait until then. Who is he, anyways?"

"He's not talking much. Did he say anything to you when you caught him?"

She thought for a moment, stroking the skin of the apple, then looked up and said, "He told me he came to town for Serial Killer Days."

Deputy Dan was running.

He was running through a cornfield on a humid summer day, the tassels whipping him across the face. His quarry was just ahead, never able to catch up, the thick wagging tail just out of reach. Nearing exhaustion, the Deputy made a lunge, tripping up the big dog, sending its fedora flying. Deputy Dan wrestled the dog onto its back, pinning it to the broken clods of mid-summer soil. The dog, whom the Deputy now recognized as McDuff the Crime Mutt, looked at him flatly, a sloppy grin on its face, and said, "My name's McDuff. What's yours?"

The Deputy smiled at McDuff, like he remembered an eight-year-old did once at a carnival. "My name's Dan."

Then the crime mutt removed a shiny object from beneath his trench coat and waved it and the Deputy felt something hot ride through his chest.

Deputy Dan woke up screaming.

Out in the park in the middle of a full moon night, a gentle breeze blowing from the direction of the sausage factory, Deputy Dan carefully broke a forked branch from a willow tree. It was too brittle and snapped in two. He tried another tree, a younger, greener tree, and broke another branch. He clasped both hands around it. The branch felt comfortable in his hands.

He went to the station, unlocked the door, and stepped inside. The moon sent a shaft of light across the floor, ending at the middle cell. Moving slowly toward the cell, the Deputy held the stick loosely, letting it point to the floor. As he neared the cell door, a line of energy seemed to travel down his arm, and the stick ascended, inch by inch, until it was pointing directly at the figure on the cot, and moved no higher. The Deputy tried to force it down, but it would not budge.

Suddenly the stick snapped in two.

The man on the cot stirred.

His heart beating wildly, something hot in his chest, the Deputy dropped the stick and raced out the door into the night, and kept running for a long time.

Monday morning came and there were no birds singing outside Debbie's window. It was hot already, the sky hazy and gray, her nightshirt sweaty under her arms and down her back. The humidity made it hard to breathe and sleep. Standing there, hands on the sill, curtains still, she thought it odd that there were no birds, and hoped that the neighbor boys hadn't been playing with their BB guns again.

"You're in the paper, dear!" Mother called out as Debbie came down to the kitchen.

"I am? Oh, that's right. I talked to Mr. Grimes at the hospital. Let me see."

Her mother handed her the latest edition of the *Standard Springs Herald*. Oh my, she thought. A big screaming banner dominated the page: "Scream Queen Silenced by Coma," held up by a slightly smaller headline: "Doctor Says She May Have Brain Murmur." Debbie scanned the story, searching for her own name, didn't find it, then saw another story with a photo snaking down the far right hand column of the paper: "There Wasn't Even Time to Say Good-bye—Rival Devastated by Queen's Illness."

"It's a very difficult time, what with my best friend laying there in a hospital bed in an unknown condition," said 18-year-old Scream Queen contestant Debbie Morning, who rushed to the hospital as soon as she found out the news.

Morning, who was with Lovey Friday night at the Dark Sky Drive-In, said she is feeling sad because it all happened so suddenly. "We never even had time to say good-bye," said Morning, dabbing a tear from her eye. . . .

"I didn't know it hit you so hard," said her mother sympathetically, touching her daughter's arm.

"He got my age right," Debbie said diplomatically.

"Well, your father was very proud."

"Has Dad's eye stopped twitching?"

"He almost looked like himself this morning. I think he worked all night again, don't even remember hearing him come to bed. He said he's got *contingency plans* ready no matter what happens with Molly."

"I wish he wouldn't get so worked up about it," said Debbie, pouring herself a glass of pure vitamin C. "It's just a parade, for goodness sake."

"It's more than that for him. You know that. He feels like the future of the town depends on him."

"Poor Dad."

Debbie finished her orange juice, and her mother asked, "Dear, could you take Bobby to the vet this morning? I promised I'd fold programs for the parade."

"To the vet, Mom?"

"Dr. Swank says he has a pill that might help him calm down. It works on dogs, he says, and what animals do little boys like to play with more?"

"Can't, Mom. I've got to go see Mrs. Toddler. In fact," she said, glancing at the clock, which read eight fifty-five, "I should be there in five minutes."

"Didn't you just have a lesson on Friday?"

"Yes, but with the pageant less than a week away, she thought it would be a good idea, give me some last minute advice and so forth."

"That's nice of her. You listen to her now, Debbie Sue. She's been to London, you know. I think she once dated a bobby."

"I like her, Mom. Gotta go." She gave her mom a peck on the cheek and left the house.

Debbie was a little nervous (but not afraid) as she biked up Vine Street to her mentor's house. She recalled that her mother had said that Mrs. Toddler's cousin Gussie had swung a dead cat at school, and this fact did not sit well with Debbie whatsoever. However, she was willing to give the woman the benefit of the doubt because Mrs. Toddler wouldn't send her to someone who was terribly mean and there was the possibility that the cat had already been dead before Gussie had started swinging it. Swinging a previously deceased cat, while not something Debbie would practice on an everyday basis, was more in the line of odd behavior than in the line of terribly mean behavior.

"Good morning, dear. So good to see you again."

"Hi, Mrs. Toddler," the somewhat edgy Debbie said, plopping down on the couch right in the middle of Niagara Falls. "How are you today?" she asked, tugging the pillow out from underneath her posterior.

"It's a sad day for all of us," said Mrs. Toddler. "Poor Molly. To think that never again may a scream be produced from that lovely throat. I didn't know she was your best friend."

"Well, we got close these past few weeks, I guess."

Holding Debbie's hand, Mrs. Toddler said, "No matter what condition she is in, try not to treat your own situation any differently. They call it a competition, but really it is each girl trying to bring out the best in herself. Remember, you have nothing to fear but fear itself."

"Hey, that's neat, Mrs. Toddler. I'll try to remember that when I'm on stage Friday night."

Smiling softly, the teacher said, "Of course, fear can be found in many places, be induced by many means."

"Your cousin."

She nodded. "Gussie."

"What's this about, Mrs. Toddler?" Debbie asked. "What is she going to do to me?"

Shaking her head, the teacher said, "It's not what she's going to do *to* you, it's what she is going to do *for* you." She handed Debbie a slip of paper with a pencil-drawn map on it. "Just follow the directions. It's not far, two miles perhaps. She's expecting you."

●

Debbie pedaled slowly down the shoulder of Route 3 to Deerhit Cutoff in the deep July heat, not knowing what to expect. Braking at the corner, she studied the map, spreading it over her handlebars. Take a left at the cutoff, right at the burned down school house, over Fairytown Creek and down the hill to a white house. A blue dragonfly landed on the hand-drawn house, wings glistening in the sun.

She shooed it away and set off again. In a short time she came upon the school house, charred timbers, burned blackboards, school's out. The trees grew more dense, hanging over the gravel road, making a cool tunnel for Debbie to ride through. Sunlight lay in patchwork across the road, gradually giving way to a solid field of shadows.

The creek appeared ahead, spanned by a bridge barely wide enough for a single car to pass. Her bicycle rattled over the rutted path, and she lost her balance for a moment, the front wheel turning to the side, but she straightened it out and hung on tight as the bike coasted down the long hill to the house of Gussie.

Debbie left her bike in the deep grass by an oak tree, its trunk the size of a barrel, and looked at the house for a moment before heading up the walk to the porch. It was an ancient, two-story dwelling, tar paper covering the upstairs windows, a half moon weather vane atop the gabled roof. The porch was sagging, the steps gray and rotted. An old crumbled bird's nest clung onto the eaves by the porch door.

She was cautious going up the steps, then opened the screen door, springs creaking, and knocked twice.

There was no answer. Suddenly she heard leaves shaking and a thud as something hit the ground behind her and a husky voice grunted and yelled out, "I'M A GONNA KILL YOU!"

Debbie turned to see what the fuss was all about. "You must be Gussie!" she said brightly.

The person who had made all the commotion was a weather-worn woman, her long gray hair hanging past her shoulders, dressed in overalls with large, fresh grass stains on both knees. The woman carefully eyed Debbie.

"My name's Debbie," said Debbie. "You're Mrs. Toddler's cousin, I understand. Well, it's very nice to meet you. Mrs. Toddler has been so nice to help me get ready for the contest, she's such a sweet person. I know you're her cousin so you probably know all this anyway, but I must say that she's the most kindest person I believe I have ever come across and I'm just so delighted to make your acquaintance."

The woman's head bobbed solemnly. "It's as she said it was," stated the woman with some wonder, "if not worse."

"What a lovely old house," Debbie remarked. "I love gables. I love birds, too. Do you have many birds?"

"Come, child," said Gussie, taking her arm. "I think I can help you."

The woman led her not into the house but around back to a small shed, red paint peeling, moss clinging to the edges of the broken shingles. The woman flipped up the wooden latch and pulled open the wobbly door. It was too dark to see much, and Gussie poked around on a shelf, picking up a small jar, which she slipped into the pocket of her overalls, and a metallic funnel-shaped can with a short length of cord dangling from one end. She shut the door and headed across the yard, Debbie trailing obediently.

They passed through a line of weeping willows, beyond which lay a garden of odd-looking black flowers and a cluster of bee-hives.

"What pretty flowers," Debbie said as the woman lit the narrow end of the funnel, smoke wafting out. "What are they?"

"I brought the originals back from the dark reaches of South Dakota long before you were even born," said Gussie. "Come, take a closer look."

They went over to the garden, bees flitting about them. The strange flowers, Debbie observed, were not all black, but had veins of red like winding country roads on a map. They smelled like incense, musky rather than sweet. Bees worked them eagerly.

"My mother never told me about flowers like this," said Debbie.

"They're very toxic, in this form," the woman said. She turned to the hives, slowly waving the funnel in a circle. "Stay back. The smoke will keep the bees calm; it confuses them, but you're still a stranger here."

Debbie did as instructed, watching as Gussie set the smoker and jar on top of a hive and removed one of the racks. A scattering of bees clung to the honeycomb. Gussie used a knife to scrape the honey into the jar, while bees crawled across her neck and down her elbow. When the jar was half filled, she screwed on the lid and returned it to her pocket. She replaced the rack and retrieved the smoker.

"Don't they sting you?" Debbie asked.

"It doesn't hurt so much," said Gussie, coming over to her. "Your body gets used to the poison. Are you afraid of bees?"

"Well, I'd rather not get stung."

"My cousin tells me you're having problems . . . with your fear."

"Yes, ma'am. I want to be Scream Queen but I'm just not convincing enough, I guess. I want to be afraid, I'm trying very hard, but who can be afraid when the world is so wonderful?" She looked up. "See how blue the sky is today? Doesn't that cloud look like a kitty playing with a ball of yarn? I think it does. And those willows, they're just the perfect creation; they're not weeping at all. Do you feel that wonderful breeze? And even the bees, they care so much about their home, they give life to the plants, humble as can be."

"Maybe you weren't meant for this. Maybe you were meant to love the clouds and nothing more."

"No," said Debbie insistently. "I've wanted to be the Scream Queen since I was a little girl and saw one walk down that aisle on pageant night. It aches inside me. I'm eighteen years old. This is my last chance. You must help me, Gussie."

"So you want to be queen bee, then."

Debbie nodded with certainty.

The old woman took the jar from her pocket and gave it to Debbie. "Then you must eat this honey."

Debbie gazed at the jar, the clumps of honey glowing in the sunshine. "It's just honey, isn't it? How could that possibly help me?"

"You must use it right, so listen to me carefully. Do not share it with anyone else. Do not use it when anyone else is around. Don't put it on bread, don't put it on anything or you will dilute the effect. Dip your fingers in it and eat it all, you must eat it all."

As they walked back under the willow trees, Debbie said, "I like honey, but what will it do to me?"

"I hope it makes you feel something you've never felt before," Gussie told her. "That is my hope."

●

When Debbie rode into the driveway at home, she hoped no one would be around, that her mother would be out folding programs, that Bobby would be getting his dog pills. But as she went into the house, there was Mom and little brother, hunched over a puzzle on the kitchen table.

"Hi, Mom!" Debbie called out, poking her head into the kitchen, honey jar on her hip.

"Hello, dear. How did it go with Mrs. Toddler today?"

"Just fine. I'm all set for Friday night. Say, Bobby seems pretty calm."

"Yes, he's my good little puppy now, aren't you, Bobby?" Mrs. Morning said, scratching behind his ear.

"Aw, Mom."

"I'm going to do some practicing in my room," Debbie said. "I'll see you guys later."

"You have fun now, dear."

Bounding up the stairs and shutting the bedroom door behind her, Debbie flopped down onto the bed, breathing a sigh of relief. She lay on her back and held the jar up with both hands, twisting it in the light. It made her feel uncomfortable to sneak something into the house, and in fact she believed this was the first time, but she didn't want to answer any questions about where she had been.

When should I eat it? Debbie wondered. Gussie said to make sure there's no one else around, so I'd better wait until everybody is in bed. That way if something embarrassing happens, like if I start bragging about myself or something, nobody else has to see it. She slid the jar under the bed. A small amount of honey which had been stuck on the outside of the jar now was clinging to her thumb. She gazed uncertainly at the sticky thumb, tempted to lick the honey off. Do I dare? she thought. This is no time to play games, she decided, and went into the bathroom and scrubbed the honey off, washing it down the drain with steaming water.

●

Debbie stayed out of sight most of the day, reading Rimbaud on the porch, tugging out weeds in the garden. After dinner she went back up to her room, a feeling of anxiousness growing as the light of day faded. Even after the sun dipped beneath the horizon, the temperature did not feel like it dropped at all, and she lifted the window as high as it would go and kept the curtains pulled apart to pick up any stray breeze possible. The old fan on the floor clattered, futilely moving the muggy air across the room.

Around ten Debbie popped back downstairs to say good night, and then returned to her room and shut the light off. She heard her mom put Bobby to bed around nine-thirty, then she came upstairs herself at about ten-fifteen and shut her door. Her dad worked late; she could hear him pacing on the wooden living room floor. Finally, just after one, his heavy, comforting footsteps sounded on the stairs and her parents' bedroom door closed for the final time that night.

Debbie waited a while longer just to be safe, then reached under her bed and pulled out the jar. The honey had taken on a darker cast now; the sunlight had made it shine golden and innocent. Propping up her pillow, Debbie sat against her headboard and unscrewed the lid. She smelled the honey, peered at it, ran her finger just on the edge of the glass, then poked her finger deep into the jar. Then two fingers were in the jar and she scooped up a clump of honey, shut her eyes, and closed her mouth over her fingers.

It tasted mostly sweet, like the good, innocent honey she had always eaten, but with a vague acrid flavor underneath the sweetness. She waited a minute, seeing if it would make her sick, and, when nothing happened, she dug in again and swallowed another mouthful, and another and soon she was wiping the bottom of the jar clean with her fingers. Her lips were sticky, wet.

Now she set the jar on the floor again and laid back on the bed. I don't feel any different, she thought.

Suddenly she heard the fluttering of wings. A bird flew into her room from the night, a grackle. It frantically made circles, and began hitting the wall opposite the window, flying into it again and again, thud, thud, thud, a blotch of blood appearing on the wall. Again and again the grackle dashed itself against the wall and then it fell dead onto the floor, black feathers floating slowly down.

Debbie sat unmoving, her mind dizzy.

The second bird found the fan to its liking.

The third bird, also a grackle, chose the wall above her bed to murder itself. Debbie covered her head, feeling warm specks spatter her arms and neck.

What's happening to me? she thought.

The fourth and fifth grackles came in together and attacked each other in the air, screeching terribly, pecking holes in each other's bodies, the blood splattering the spiraling, grinning suns on her bedspread. One mutilated bird lay convulsing on the foot of the bed, the other was dead on the floor. Debbie clamped her eyes shut, violently shaking her head. "No!" she yelled. She heard more fluttering, the room filling with birds, the bodies thudding against the wall, the warm wetness enveloping her, screeching, feathers on her lips, stuck in the honey and blood.

"NO!" she screamed.

There was a rush of silence.

Heart pounding, she slowly opened her eyes.

The room was empty, clean. It was light out, the sun streaming through the window. She went over and looked outside.

There were grackles everywhere, hundreds of them. On the ground, in the trees, crowded together on the telephone wires. They were not singing or looking for food or even moving. They seemed to be waiting.

Then a grackle landed on the sill, not a foot from Debbie's hand.

"Maybe you weren't meant for this," said the grackle sincerely.

They gazed at one another for a long moment, bird and girl, then the grackle hopped about, facing the other grackles. They began screeching again, a glorious chorus. He took off, and the multitude of grackles followed his lead, turning the sky into a black cloud that rose above the trees and swept back over the house.

Debbie sat down on her bed. She used the sleeve of her nightshirt to wipe the residue of honey from her mouth, then she curled up and fell asleep as darkness filled her room again and the ancient fan clattered on into the night.

7

Deputy Dan avoided the jailhouse early on Monday morning. He patrolled Main Street, played with a dog in the park, grabbed a mug of coffee at the diner. Around nine he took the squad car and drove out to the Flatwire place.

Mrs. Flatwire was in her orchard, poking a thermometer into the soil beneath each tree and peering at the reading. The Deputy caught up to her midway down one of the rows.

"Mornin', Mrs. Flatwire," the Deputy said at some distance so not to startle her, although he did not see her rifle nearby.

"Good morning, Deputy," replied the apple woman, a placid expression on her tanned face. "It's a fine morning, don't you think?"

"Yes, ma'am, it certainly is."

"Thank you again for returning my gun. I didn't mean to be so huffy the other day. It's not usually my way, it's just that my babies were being threatened, you understand."

"Yes, ma'am, I understand that," Deputy Dan said. "In fact, that's why I'm here. I wanted to make sure you still were willing to press charges against that fella who trespassed. If you don't decide to press charges against him today, we'll be forced to release him."

"Press charges? Goodness, no. Let the poor boy go. He had no way of knowing he was traipsing through the greatest apple orchard in the state."

The Deputy swallowed hard.

"We must all try to get along in this world," Mrs. Flatwire said with finality.

"I d-d-don't think that would be a very good idea."

"I just want to drop the whole thing," she said. "Why ruin a perfectly good morning?"

Looking away, a line of sweat forming above his upper lip, Deputy Dan said quietly, "You know, ma'am, I've been a deputy in this town for a long while, seen a lot of things. I know how people are. You have to believe me, Mrs. Flatwire, that if we start getting soft on criminal activity in Standard Springs, before long we're going to have a first-rate crime spree on our hands; and people will wonder how it all began and I'll have to say, 'I *told* Mrs. Flatwire to press charges against that trespasser.' Oh, it's classic. Go up to PowPow Penitentiary and talk to your hardened criminal and you'll see exactly what I'm talking about. All those lifers didn't begin their careers with raping and killing. No, ma'am, it was apple stealing, trespassing, that sort of thing. One day a kid is stealing apples and the next day he's breaking into your house and stealing your life savings out of your piano. If we don't take a stand from the start with those who break the law, we'll be neck deep in dead bodies before long. Do you understand what I mean, Mrs. Flatwire?"

The Deputy turned to her.

"Mrs. Flatwire?"

Where was she?

Crouched under a tree some distance away, the apple woman pulled her thermometer from the soil, nodded, and moved on to the next tree.

The Deputy left the orchard, walking quickly back around the house to his squad car. Before getting in he leaned against the hood, head down, until the dizzy feeling went away.

●

Driving by Victory Park on the way back to headquarters, Deputy Dan noticed that it was the scene of some activity. Junior Sasser again, but this time he was not alone in the park. Down at the far end of the park what appeared to be a pale green flying saucer skimmed low over the grass. The Deputy parked by the ball field and walked over to Junior.

"Hey, Junior. Find anything yet?"

"Not yet," said Junior, keeping a close watch on the end of his dowsing stick. "I'm expectin' to feel that vibration any minute now, though."

"If your brother doesn't find it first."

An angry look crossed his face. "My brother! Don't even tell me about him."

"That's some contraption he's got there. Did he make it himself?"

"Make it himself? With his money? He went up to Bald Lake, got it from some trailer salesmen, Army surplus from what I hear. They used it to locate land mines in some war or t'other."

Hands on his hips, the Deputy shook his head and said, "Whew, that's some slick machine. How are you ever going to beat something like that?"

"Because I have the righteous will of Nature on my side. I'm connected to the earth, don't you see? A direct line. What can you find with a heap like his, all metal and wires and numbers? Not what we're lookin' for, that's for certain."

The saucer hummed by them. His brother Leon waved and grinned at them from under the bubble. Deputy Dan waved back.

"I tried dowsing something the other night," the Deputy said. "I . . . something happened. I found something, although I'm not sure what yet."

Junior stopped and looked at him. "What were you huntin' for, Deputy?"

"I . . . I don't know. The stick went crazy. It was like an electric shock. The stick snapped in two, right in my hands."

Junior whistled. "You have encountered some kinda powerful force. Mebbe we're gonna get an earthquake. What was in your mind?"

"I can't tell you. I'm sorry."

"The thing that was in your mind, did you find that?"

"I think so."

"Were your thoughts clear and were you focusin' in?"

"I'm not sure. It was so confusing."

Sighing, Junior said, "You shoulda come to me first. I coulda showed you the book. We coulda done it right. Do you wanna try again? I'll help you."

"No, we can't do it now," said the Deputy. He looked helplessly at Junior. "What do you think it was?"

Junior spit on the ground and said, "Well, I don't know if you found what you were lookin' for, but you sure as heck found somethin', and whatever it is I wouldn't mess with it if I was you."

Just then the hovercraft came past and stopped, the motor winding down into silence. A paunchy red-haired man in Bermuda shorts and a Hawaiian shirt exited from a rear hatch, followed by a white bulldog.

"Howdy, fellas," he said jovially. "I hope you aren't looking for the prize, because you're not going to find it in this park."

"What makes you so dang sure about that?" Junior asked.

"The Soil Sonar doesn't lie," he said. "I'm going to finish all the parks in town by lunch and do the fairgrounds this afternoon and I bet you anything I'll find the prize and still be home in time for dinner."

"Oh, go to heck right now," Junior said with a disgusted wave of the hand, and stormed off.

"Come on, bro, don't be such a spoil sport," Leon called after him. "You want a ride on the saucer? Let's go for a ride on the saucer, whaddaya say?"

Junior kept going, dowsing stick bobbing up and down.

"Why did he get so hot?" Leon asked Deputy Dan. "I was just trying to have fun. Why does he have to take it so seriously?"

"When was the last time he won?" the Deputy said.

"The last time Junior won? Oh, geez, I don't know, it's been years. I can't help it if I'm a better treasure hunter than him. What am I supposed to do, pretend I can't find it? He wouldn't respect me if I did that, not that he respects me now."

"He really wants to find it this year, Leon."

"Well, so do I. But is it my fault that he never amounted to much? We started out the same, you know, we are brothers. There's no reason why we both couldn't be riding around the park in hovercrafts. No reason at all. I worked a lot of long nights making the Burgerama what it is today. I could have been a switchman for the railroad, too, but I wanted more out of life."

"I like Burgerama," said the Deputy. "The vanilla shakes are good."

"This is just a friendly competition. If he makes any more of it than that, well, then that's his problem." Leon strode testily back to the saucer and climbed inside. It did a loop and headed back to the other end of the park where his trailer was parked.

Deputy Dan started back to the Sheriff's office. When he reached the corner he hesitated in front of Raisin Implement, which was directly across the street from their office. He stared at the jailhouse for some time.

Are you the killer? Are you the killer? Deputy Dan repeated again and again in his head, holding his hands out, trying to feel that special feeling again.

8

Serial Killer Days officially began Monday afternoon with the 5K Run for Your Life. There was also a 1K Run for Your Life, Kids for those in the twelve and under set. The race route began at Kraven Park and wound through the center of town, reaching the midway point out by the junkyard, then circling back down Main Street and finally returning to the park and the finish line. Usually some member of the track team won; last year it was nervous Jeffy Deel, who beat the course record with a stunning time of 25:41.

There was another fine turnout this year, Arvid Morning noticed, as he strode through the park. The participants were stretching and running in place and adjusting their bibs at the starting line. Some were dressed in bright track shorts and fishnet shirts, others just had on jeans and sneakers. Some of the bodies were lean and taut, others were products of Weed's Bakery. Arvid had important matters to attend to, like clown deployment strategy, but since the race was the inaugural event of Serial Killer Days, it was traditional for the town's leading lights to pay their respects.

"Morning, Arv," Mayor Sellit said, twirling the starting gun on his index finger. "Lovely day for a race, isn't it?"

"Beautiful," Arvid agreed, stifling a yawn.

"Late night, eh?"

"It was my turn to hide the treasure hunt prize. I felt like a spy. I'm positive nobody saw me, though."

Sidling up close, the Mayor whispered, with a fraternal grin, "So where did you hide it?"

"Why, Mayor, I'm surprised you'd even ask such a question."

"At the fairgrounds, right? Is that where it is?"

"You'll have to get a shovel, Mayor, like everyone else."

"I just may do that!" the Mayor said, chuckling. His expression turned serious. "No problem getting a proper prize, I take it."

"No. The medical school had some nice selections this year."

"We're ready to go, Mr. Mayor!" someone called out.

"Hang around after the start," the Mayor told Arvid. "I need to talk to you about something." He broke away and headed over to the starting line, which was actually just the general area around Ol' Oakie.

"Okay, now, is everybody ready?"

"Yaahh!" the runners yelled.

"I want a fair race out there today. No jostling, no pushing, no punching, no cutting in front of other runners. There's a water station at the junkyard if you get dried out. Have a good race and we'll see you back here soon!"

The Mayor held the starting pistol up high. "Runners on your mark!"

They hunched over, frozen.

"Get set!"

The Mayor dropped into a firing stance, aiming at the backs of the runners. "GO!" he shouted, shooting the starting pistol three times in quick succession.

They leapt off the starting line, hollering and screaming, and soon were on the street heading toward the heart of town.

The kids lined up next. The Mayor only fired twice at them.

Once the excitement had died down, Arvid walked with the Mayor back to their cars. "I had a call from Judge Flail this morning," said the Mayor. "He says we've got a new possibility for our guest of honor. They brought him in on Friday. Out of towner. Won't talk much about himself. Scruffy-looking fellow, I guess. Smart mouth."

"What did they nab him for?"

"Trespassing. Mrs. Flatwire caught him in her apple orchard."

"And he's still around to talk about it?"

"I guess it was a pretty tense scene. You can imagine."

"And she's going to press charges?"

"She's going to today, from what I hear. Shouldn't be a problem, the way she reacted."

"That's good. I didn't care for the DWI. Too lackadaisical to be believable."

"The Judge wants us to meet with the prisoner this afternoon. We can do it now, if you're free."

Nodding, Arvid said, "That would be fine. The sooner we take care of it the better."

●

The meeting was held in a spare room in the basement of the courthouse. When Arvid Morning and Mayor Sellit entered the room, Judge Flail and Sheriff Eeha were already there, standing beside a table where a dark-eyed man was seated, leaning back in his chair, the look in his eyes an odd mixture of puzzlement and bemusement.

"Thanks for coming, boys," said the Judge. "I'd like to introduce you to Mr. Samuel Centaur." He chummily placed his hands on the prisoner's shoulders. "Well, what do you think of him? Isn't he a winner?"

"Stand up," Arvid instructed the man.

The apple thief gave them a long, sweeping glance, then slowly rose.

"Now turn around."

The man did as he was told.

Scrutinizing him carefully, Arvid said, nodding, "He's certainly got the Look."

"Can I sit down again?" the man asked.

"Feel free," said Arvid.

"Now, Sam, I suppose you're wondering why an unrefined, apple stealing fella like yourself is getting all this attention from

Standard Springs' best and brightest," said the Judge, circling around to the front of the table.

"The thought had crossed my mind," the man concurred.

"You understand you have serious charges pending against you, correct?"

"I know I was arrested. I don't reckon I know how serious the charges are, your honor."

"Well then allow me to inform you, sir. You've got one count of aggravated trespassing and two counts of felonious damage to property, by which I mean Mrs. Flatwire's cherished and prize-winning apples."

"I only ate a teensy couple bites out of one apple," the thief argued. "Besides, it had a worm in it."

"Now, we could make it three counts if you continue with that kind of slander," the Judge said.

"Four, if you count resisting arrest," the Sheriff chimed in.

"I didn't resist nothing," said the man. "I went along peaceful-like. Ask your Deputy."

"Look, boy, don't tell me how to do my job," warned the Sheriff, his jaw jutting out.

"The point is," said the Judge, "you're in a bit of a spot here, son. You're at least looking at a couple-hundred-dollar fine, which is more than carrying around money by the looks of you, maybe thirty days in jail, maybe some community service. Depends on your willingness to cooperate with the court."

"Let's hear it, your holiness. What do you fellas want from me?"

The Judge looked at his comrades, then returned his gaze to the apple thief. "What if I told you there was a way out of this mess that wouldn't involve a fine or jail time and would get you out of town by the end of the week?"

"I'm listening."

"There's something we want you to do. It's in the community service area. Not hard labor, in fact you'll be handsomely honored. You'll be a privileged guest."

"Sounds good so far."

"You know what this week is?" the Judge asked.

"It's Serial Killer Days. Everybody knows that."

"You've been here before then?" inquired Arvid. "For the celebration, I mean."

"Naw, just heard stuff about it. Wanted to see it firsthand."

"But you've been to Standard Springs before," Arvid said.

"Just on a passing-through basis."

"Any friends or relatives in town?"

"Nope."

"Any reason to think anyone would recognize you?"

"Just you folks and the apple queen."

"We'll handle her," the Judge said. "Now, as you may know, the highlight of Serial Killer Days comes Saturday night when we present our Parade of Fear. The focus of the parade is the Scream Queen float. On that float are the Scream Queen contestants and a cage inhabited by what we tell folks is a one hundred percent certified serial killer. Beauty and the beast kinda deal, see? The crowd eats it up."

"I can imagine," said the prisoner.

"It's done very tastefully," added Arvid.

The Judge looked at the apple thief with a shy, first-date look in his eyes. "Sam," he said in a small voice, "would you please be our serial killer?"

·

THE OLE RIMBAUD EXPERIENCE

·

Why, if it isn't Molly Lovey's best pal!"

Debbie hesitated as she approached the stage in the high school gymnasium. Her fellow contestants were stretching, doing practice leaps, standing around and chatting, all dressed in black leotards and T-shirts.

Samantha Sink stood leering at the stage edge, holding a copy of the *Standard Springs Herald.* "And you never even had time to say good-bye. That's really sad."

"I didn't say any of those things, Samantha," said Debbie, pulling herself up onto the stage.

"Nice picture, too. How much did you pay him to put it on the front page?"

"I didn't pay anybody anything."

"Or maybe I should ask how much he paid you."

"You be quiet!" Debbie said angrily, swatting at the newspaper.

The other girls broke off their conversations and warm-ups and began to gather around.

"You're really playing dirty," said Samantha. "I can't believe you did it."

"What are you talking about?" Debbie asked.

"Less than a week before the pageant and here you are on the front page of the paper, with a picture and everything, telling the whole town you're Molly's best friend. You aren't her best friend at all. You think she's as much of a snob as the rest of us do."

"Yeah, Deb," said Tabby. "What about that?"

"But I told you I didn't say any of those things!" Debbie exclaimed, tears starting to build up.

"You lied so you'd look good in the judges' eyes," Samantha continued. "Get the whole town on your side."

"*I did not.*" Debbie's breathing was coming in heaves now. "My . . . my dad said I should go look for her on Saturday. Remember? All you guys heard that, didn't you? I didn't know where to start looking for her. She wasn't at home or anything so I went uptown and ran into Mr. Grimes and he told me she was in the hospital so I went with him and he asked me questions about her and I didn't really say too much but I didn't say any of those things he said I did. I really didn't!"

"Oh, *right,*" said Samantha, rolling her eyes.

"I didn't tell him to put my picture on the front page," Debbie said pleadingly. "I would never do that. If I win, I want it to be fair and square."

"Well, you have zero chance to win," Samantha snapped. "I don't care if you're on the front page or not. You're over the hill. If you were going to win you would've won by now. You're just not afraid enough. A happy-go-lucky person is what you are. Happy-go-lucky."

Debbie stared at Samantha, her cheeks flushing. Then she quickly brought her hand back and slapped her competitor hard across the jaw. Samantha's head jerked to the side.

Samantha held a hand to her cheek, wincing in pain. When she lowered it, her perfect alabaster skin was marred by a red blotch shaped like the state of Texas.

The girls gasped in horror.

"Oh my gosh," said Debbie, covering her mouth. "I didn't mean it. Are you okay?" She tried to touch Samantha's arm, but Samantha pushed her hand away.

"Good morning, girls!" came a deep threatening voice from the other end of the gym. "Stop standing around and get ready to work! Move it! Move it! Move it!"

Penelope Exeter, the stout pageant show director and prison guard at PowPow Penitentiary, had arrived, putting an end to the confrontation. She hopped up onto the stage in one easy motion. "That's some welt there, Sink," she said, poking the blotch with the end of her billy club, which she employed as a baton, among other things. "Nice touch."

Now addressing the whole group, gesturing with the club, she said, "This is the kind of creative thinking I like to see. The experience I can lend you girls will only take you so far. To truly make this a memorable show for the audience, you must bring your own innate creativity into play. Samantha's injury here may seem like a small touch, perhaps only a handful of audience members will take note of it, but it is the accumulation of such effects that lifts a show from the humdrum to something people will remember for many years to come."

"What can we do if we don't want to get hit in the face?" asked Lois Langtry, who was making her first appearance in the pageant.

"Well, a few stitches would be nice, or a black eye," said Penelope. "It really depends on the individual."

"I wouldn't mind getting slugged in the arm," Lois opined.

"That would work fine. Just make sure the gown you'll be wearing won't hide the scars. And don't be too obvious about showing it off to the audience. The judges don't like that. They like that element of surprise. Nothing impresses the judges more than hearing a gasp from the crowd when they see a long, angry gash across the beautiful, tender back of a contestant."

"Does it matter how fresh it looks?" asked Tabby.

"Absolutely. The fresher the better. An old wound is like last year's gown. Unfortunately, Miss Sink here may see her pride and joy fade into meaninglessness in a day or two, from the looks of it. She may want to get hit in the same spot on Thursday afternoon or evening."

"When *is* the best time to get marked up?" Lois asked.

"That's a difficult question to answer. Again, it depends on the individual situation. For superficial wounds, waiting until Friday afternoon would not be out of the question. However, if you undergo an injury that results in trauma or shock, it is probably wise not to wait until the last minute, because you still need to be at your best for the judges' questioning and the talent portion of the pageant."

"Can't we just use paint or makeup or something to make it *look* like a laceration?" Lois asked.

"Squeamish, eh? Well, let me tell you something, young lady: There are no shortcuts up the ladder of success. Even if the audience is fooled, the judges won't be. They've seen it all over the years, all the little tricks, all the little games. If just one judge notices, your chances of becoming Scream Queen are between slim and none and slim just got disemboweled. I know it seems tempting, but trust me that it's simply not worth it."

"Do you think Molly tried to hurt herself?" asked Debbie.

Penelope thought for a moment, then said, "I'm not sure. You wouldn't think she would need to, considering her history of success in the pageant. But you never know. Maybe she didn't want to take a chance. Whatever the case, she certainly went overboard and I would not recommend you trying to duplicate her feat. I don't know if she's even awake yet. Has anybody heard anything?"

Nobody said a word.

"Perhaps you should all visit her after practice and give her your best wishes and thoughts, even if she can't hear you."

Silence again.

"Just a friendly suggestion in the spirit of comradeship," the prison guard said. "Now, are there any other questions before we begin? No? All right, today we will revisit our opening number. We were a little sloppy last time, girls, so we need to tighten up and concentrate and all work together. In a very few days this gym will be packed with your friends and relatives watching your every move and we don't want to disappoint them now, do we? Do we?"

"No, ma'am!" they called out in unison.

"So line up back in the wings, girls, and take it from the top."

Finding her place at the left rear of the stage behind the curtain, Debbie said to Samantha, who stood just off to her side, "I truly didn't mean to hurt you, Samantha. I just got so mad. I hardly said anything to Mr. Grimes. You have to believe me."

"I don't care about that, and besides, it didn't even hurt that much," Samantha said.

"I'm *really, really* sorry."

"I don't want to talk to you."

"But we have to work together, even if you're mad at me for now," said Debbie hopefully.

"Just stay away from me."

"I know, I'll call the paper, have Mr. Grimes tell you it wasn't the way he said it was. He just made a mistake, that's all. Everybody makes mistakes."

"Shhh," someone hissed.

"Here we go!" Penelope called out from the foot of the stage. "Listen for your cue!"

The taped music began, trumpets blaring a fanfare. The girls hushed, waiting.

The music stopped. A low, menacing laugh sounded. Then a syncopated synthesized beat began, and the contestants shimmied out from behind the curtains.

"Who will it be, who will it be?" they sang, pointing threatening fingers at the imaginary audience. *"Maybe you, or you, or maybe ME!"*

"Make sure you wait until the ME to point your finger at yourself," corrected Miss Exeter. "Not on the MAYBE! The gesture should be a surprise to the audience and appear to be a surprise to you as well!"

"Oh, he's coming to town, that man we've all been waiting for, that man with the terrible frown, oh yes he's coming to town!"

"Look around now, look around, like he could jump out from behind the curtains at any moment!"

The girls swung around into a row and began high-kicking. Debbie, still upset, just went through the motions.

"With a glint in his eye and a gleam in his knife, he might come looking for you, he might take your life!"

"Nice work!" Penelope called out, smiling with satisfaction. "You girls could all get jobs at PowPow with that kind of kicking!"

They finished the run-through of the opening number, then Miss Exeter gathered the contestants around her in a semicircle and said, "We've come a long way in the past few weeks, ladies. There are a few rough edges, there always are, but we'll clean up those areas in the next couple days and be ready to present a fine show for the folks on Friday. Any questions on the opening number? Otherwise, we'll move on to the 'Mr. Mayhem' sequence."

"I have a question!" Lois the greenhorn said, raising her hand. "Yes, Lois."

"Is Kirk Potz really going to sing with us?" she asked.

"Yes, he will, Lois," said Penelope. "In fact, he'll be coming in later this week to rehearse with us, provided his parole officer has no objections."

The girls shivered.

"What a nightmare," Lois cooed.

Debbie wrinkled her nose, but didn't say anything. She did not care for the crooner and felon from East Fill, who could be seen every Saturday night on KTBB-TV's *Bandwagon* show. He was too smarmy and looked like a troublemaker to boot. Of all the *Bandwagon* singers, she favored Archy Loss, the great barber shop soloist. When he sang "Eileen of the Eire" she felt weak in her knees. She had even written him a fan letter once, and he sent her back a glossy photograph signed, *"To Debbie, my #1 fan, A big Bandwagon hug to you, Archy."*

"Please, girls," said Miss Exeter, "when Mr. Potz arrives, try not to fawn all over him. Be professional. We won't have much time to rehearse with him, so we must be efficient."

"I can hardly wait," said Lois with a sigh.

●

After practice, Debbie found an empty corner of the stage and wiped the sweat from her face with a towel, keeping her head down. She didn't feel like talking to anybody, and was glad that no one had sought her out. Now that she had a chance to cool down, she recognized that while it was not fair that her fellow contestants, especially Samantha, had treated her with so much distrust, she also knew that her own reaction may not have been any different had their roles been reversed. They were all victims of a careless newspaperman. Or was it just carelessness? Did Griff Grimes have another motive for making up those quotes? Debbie's immediate reaction, as usually was the case, was to give him the benefit of the doubt. Gosh, he probably worked all night, or couldn't read his own handwriting, I've sure done that before, and he tried to string her words together the best way he could remember.

But the more she thought about it, the madder she became. He should have at least called me before he ran the story and asked if he got my words right, she decided.

"Anything wrong, Miss Morning?"

Debbie looked up. It was the instructor. "No, ma'am."

"You looked a little lifeless out there."

As she was about to offer an excuse, Penelope Exeter winked at her and said, "Good job."

●

Knowing her mood would soften if she waited much longer, Debbie headed down to the newspaper office on the way home from practice. She rang the bell on the counter, and shortly Randy Reeds, a jovial fellow with a crewcut and a T-shirt with a tie painted onto it, came out front. He was the sports guy, and when she had been a football cheerleader, she had watched in amazement as he trudged up and down the sidelines following the ball in rain, sleet, snow and even after he broke a foot and was hobbling around in a cast. She liked him just fine.

"Hey, Deb!" he greeted her. "How are you doing?"

"Just swell, Randy. How are you?"

"Doing great, doing great."

"Say, who won the Run for Your Life yesterday?"

"Jeffy Deel, again! I've never seen anyone look so nervous. When that gun sounded, whoosh," he made an upward swooping motion with his hand, "he took off flying. He knocked a couple seconds off last year's record."

Peeking behind him down the corridor leading to the newspaper's offices, Debbie said, "Is Mr. Grimes around?"

"Sure," Randy said with a wave. "Come on back."

She followed him down the hallway to a small, cluttered office. The editor was hunched over his computer, two fingers pounding the keyboard. Randy tapped on the door frame. "Someone here to see you, stud."

The editor flapped his hand in response. "He'll be right with you," Randy said, and went into an adjacent office.

After a moment Griff Grimes gave the keyboard one last jab, then swiveled around in his chair. "Ah, Miss Morning. How is the front-page girl today?"

"Lousy," she said. "I have a bone to pick with you, Mr. Grimes."

He looked at her curiously for a second, then said, "Close the door and have a seat."

After pulling the door shut and sitting down self-consciously, she brought her eyes to his and said, "That wasn't a very nice thing to do, Mr. Grimes."

"It wasn't? What wasn't?"

"Saying I said those things when I didn't."

"Which things?"

Seeing a copy of the notorious paper on his desk, she picked it up and waved it in his face. "All of it!"

"You're saying I misquoted you?"

"People are accusing me of pretending to be Molly's best

friend so I'll win the pageant. I never told you I was her best friend. I never told you *any* of this."

"Well, I tried to re-create our conversation as best as I could. Taking notes really isn't my strong suit. I have trouble reading my own handwriting, to tell you the truth. I should learn short-hand someday, there just doesn't seem to be time."

"That doesn't do me any good now. They all hate me."

"Why, I thought you'd be thrilled to be on the front page of the paper. Not many people get that honor, you know."

"I do know, and I wish you would have saved that honor for somebody else. I want to win fair and square. I don't need any help."

Rocking back and forth in his chair, the springs creaking, Grimes said, "That's not what I've heard."

"What are you talking about? What have you heard?"

"Debbie Morning, the Girl Without Fear. A bit of a handicap for someone who wants to be Scream Queen, don't you think?"

Looking down at her black sneakers, Debbie said quietly, "You should mind your own business, Mr. Grimes."

"You're going to have to learn these things if you intend on staying in Standard Springs, or Serial Killer, as they're planning to call it."

She lifted her head. "They're changing the name of the town?"

"It's a lock, once they look at the finances involved. How is a happy camper like you going to survive here?"

"I'll fit in. Some people are slow learners, that's all."

"You really want to be Scream Queen, don't you?"

She nodded emphatically. "More than anything."

Leaning back in his chair, hands locked behind his head, he rocked slightly and said, "I may be able to help you."

"You've made a mess of things for me so far."

"I want to make amends."

"You're thinking about something. What is it?"

"Have you ever been to the Cities?"

"We took a field trip there once in grade school. I remember seeing a mummy at the science museum."

Gazing at her seriously, he said, "Have you ever been in the midtown area at about three in the morning?"

"No, of course not."

"I could take you there. You might find what you're looking for. In fact, I would say the odds would be pretty favorable."

Debbie did not say anything. The proposal hung there in midair, her mind tentatively reaching out toward it.

"You're eighteen years old," he said. "You're an adult, not a girl anymore."

"I don't know," she finally said. "I've never done anything like that before. The Cities . . . It's such a big place. . . ."

"We can go tonight. I've got to take a picture down at the fire station at seven, then I'm interviewing Karen Mon . . . Mon something, who just had a wisdom tooth removed, and Dr. Temblor says it's the smartest wisdom tooth he's ever seen. Great feature story. Leave a little time to write up my notes . . . hmm. How does nine o'clock grab you?"

"I . . . I don't know. I have to think about this. What would I tell my parents?"

"You've never snuck out of the house before?"

"Well, no, not exactly. I went to a slumber party once, though."

He swiveled his chair back to the computer and resumed his typing. "Forget I said anything. I'm sorry I messed up your quotes. It won't happen again."

"But if I want to go you'll be here at nine, right?"

He didn't answer her.

"I guess I'll go now," she said quietly, getting up. "Thank you for your time." She hurriedly left the newspaper office.

●

Remembering Miss Exeter's suggestion, Debbie made a brief side trip on the way home. She rode over to Standard Springs Memorial Hospital, left her bicycle at the entrance, and went inside.

Debbie found Molly's room, peeking in before entering. Her rival was alone and still. Debbie went to the bed, careful not to make a sound, although, she thought, if Molly is in a coma, she probably wouldn't notice me even if I made a horrible racket, not that I would, of course.

Pulling a chair up to the bed and sitting down, Debbie couldn't get over how helpless and innocent Molly appeared to be. Her face was plain and clean, her hair flat, her attire the basic blue and white patient gown, not some designer hospital dress.

I've never really given her much consideration, Debbie thought. I always kept my distance, thinking she was so perfect and snooty, hating her for it, believing the worst of her at all times. Debbie felt peer pressure from the other girls to give Molly the cold shoulder, unspoken yet very real, but now that she was on the outs she didn't feel that pressure anymore.

Debbie squeezed her rival's hand. It was warm, and not at all snooty. "I hope you get better," she said to her softly. "I really do."

•

As Debbie biked home her thoughts returned to Mr. Grimes's offer. Can I really go to the Cities? The idea doesn't make me afraid, she thought, just mildly uneasy. She recalled a story her mother told her once about an unidentified cousin who went to the Cities and never came back. Her not coming back was related with such an ominous cast that Debbie had imagined all sorts of things. Maybe she was discovered by some big television producer who put her on the first plane to California. Maybe she was run down by a taxi cab. Or maybe the city just swallowed her up whole.

Is that what fear is? Debbie wondered. The not knowing, the idea that everything isn't planned and choreographed, that the possibilities are boundless and that anything can happen to you? She found this thought to be a little far-fetched but interesting. It was like Ole Rimbaud wrote: "Hogs may be men / in some starry worlds."

But shouldn't the Cities be the same as Standard Springs, only bigger? People lived there, people just like my friends and neighbors. They worked and raised families and went to slumber parties. It seemed chaotic from the outside, but the people who lived there were probably just as regular as the people living in my town. It was just easier to get lost in the Cities, that's all. Maybe that's what Mr. Grimes meant. Getting lost could be pretty scary.

But I'm not lost now! she thought, trying to cheer herself up. There was her house, the same house she had lived in for all of her eighteen years. The same white gate, the same sidewalk where she skinned her knee as a kid. Still got the scar, too. Nothing that would impress Miss Exeter, certainly, but she was proud of it in an odd sort of way, a link to the naive kid she used to be.

Leaving her bike by the front step, Debbie went into the house. Her mother was on the phone in the kitchen. When she saw Debbie, she pressed the receiver to her chest. "It's your father. The usual countdown panic. How are you, dear? How was rehearsal?"

"Great, Mom. Say, Miss Exeter's got a big slumber party planned for all the contestants tonight, she's big on that camaraderie junk. We're going to play games and make cookies and stuff. Can I go?"

"Certainly, dear. Be sure and pack your toothbrush."

"Thanks, Mom. Say hi to Dad for me." Debbie ran upstairs, feeling the blood pumping through her body. I don't like lying, she thought, but I don't want them to worry. I'm eighteen now, and I have to take responsibility for myself.

"Hey!"

Debbie pulled up short as she reached the top of the stairway. "Sorry, kid. What are you up to?"

Bobby started barking, then got down on all fours, blocking her progress. "I wanna go to the rides! You said!"

"I didn't forget, shorty. We'll go tomorrow night. Roger will be there, too. It'll be fun."

"Can I go on all the rides?"

"Well, maybe not on all of them. Some of the rides are just for big kids, you know."

"I'm a big dog!" he said, hopping up.

"Ask Mother, then."

"When's Anti Claus coming?"

"Not for a few days yet. You'll just have to wait.".

"He can't get me, I'm the biggest dog ever!" Bobby yelled, and bounded down the stairs.

Debbie went to her room. She changed into her cheer squad T-shirt, then lay on her bed and read Ole Rimbaud for a while, and was dozing off when the telephone roused her.

"Debbie dear! Roger's on the phone!"

Shaking the fuzz from her mind, Debbie grabbed the receiver.

"Hey, peanut pumpkin."

"Hi, boyfriend. Whatcha doing?"

"Don't tell the gang, but my knees are shakin' like a dog."

"What's wrong?"

"Opening night jitters, I guess," he said. "Won't get too bad, though, knowin' my girl will be out there in the audience. I'll just look down at you and you can give me a little smile, and things will be A-OK."

"Tonight?"

"Yeah, it seems like just yesterday that we started practicin'. I got my grunt down good, though. Do you wanna hear it? Okay, here she comes with the club, sneaking up behind me. She swings! UUUUNNNNNHH!!!"

There was silence on the line.

"So what do you think?"

"Uh, that's great, Rog."

Gosh darn it! Debbie swore to herself. How could I have forgotten about the musical?

"I've got a ticket reserved for you," he said. "I had to pull a few strings, but you're going to be right up in the front row. You don't have to thank me. You know that I'd do anything for you, baby."

"Uh, thanks Rog."

"I gotta go now. I need to rehearse my line some more."

Debbie hung up the phone, the grunts cut off suddenly, and sat back on the bed in a daze. What a fix, she thought. I can't miss the musical, but Mr. Grimes is offering to open a door for me that I can't refuse to pass through. Shoot, usually Serial Killer

Days is so *predictable*. There must be a way out of this jam.

Debbie set her mind to figuring out the solution. She sat on her bed for some time, counting down to nightfall, waiting for the dark and whatever may come.

Excitement ran feverishly through town on Wednesday evening, along with a good measure of dread, as theatergoers flocked to the high school for opening night of *The Sound of Maniacs*. The school parking lot filled up early, and the side streets soon were jammed with autos, too. As Debbie biked up Nickerson Street to the school, she saw that some kids had set up a lemonade stand in their yard and seemed to be doing good business on this sultry night. She slowly weaved among the knots of people walking along, trying to keep her story straight in her mind. An amateur at concocting and managing stories, she kept reminding herself who should be told what.

Roger. Felt a little faint and had to leave. You did a great job, though, sweets.

Mom and Dad. Went to Miss Exeter's house right after the play. Had a fine time. You'll enjoy the show. Roger did a terrific job.

The other contestants. Oh, mind your own darn business, but if you must know Rog did a wonderful job.

Was that everybody? Who else did she need to tell a fib? Well, that was certainly enough people to lie to for one night, she thought. She realized the only person who would know the real truth would be Mr. Grimes.

Debbie locked up her bike on a railing outside the main entrance to the school and joined the throngs streaming inside the building. After picking up her ticket at the window, she entered the half-filled auditorium, going down the center aisle to find her seat. What did the ticket say? A7. She studied the chair arms, counting them off, then sat down in the front row, off to the right of center stage. She slouched down in her seat, trying to look inconspicuous, not wanting to meet anyone she would have to add to her Big Fat Lie List.

Soon the auditorium filled up and the house lights dimmed. Mrs. Toddler, who had adapted the musical for Serial Killer Days, took her place at the piano down on the far end of the stage. The curtain opened, the music began, and the performers launched into their first number.

"The hills are alive . . ."

Just before the opening song ended, *Herald* sports editor Randy Reeds snuck down to the front of the auditorium, snapped a few pictures, then retreated back up the aisle.

Debbie watched with less than complete interest, having seen the play many times before and being preoccupied with her own machinations. Even so, she had to smile and mouth the words when the performers sang her best-loved songs, like "My Wonderful Things."

"Blood drops on noses and deep gaping gashes / girls in white dresses with gouges and slashes / poor helpless victims tied up with string / these are a few of my wonderful things . . ."

The adapted plot told the story of a large family living in Switzerland whose military father hires a governess to take care of his children. Things start out fine, until the children begin to die mysteriously. All fingers point to the governess and the action escalates until the emotional climatic battle where the father and the governess battle to the death with chain saws.

Debbie figured Roger would be making his appearance soon. He played an innocent bystander who gets thunked on the head by the governess when he accidentally bumps into her at the market. Glancing at her watch, Debbie sure hoped it would be soon. It was already 8:45. It would probably take her a good ten minutes to get from the school to the Herald. What if Mr. Grimes had forgotten, she thought, or worse yet, hadn't taken me seriously?

I shouldn't have been so darn wishy-washy. Debbie fidgeted in her seat.

Finally, the governess, played by bank teller Genevieve Gossamer, had taken her basket and was heading for the door!

The curtain came down. There was a rustling backstage, Debbie could see many sets of feet scurrying about beneath the gap at the bottom of the curtain. A few moments later the curtain rose again, revealing a warmly lit town square scene. There was Rog, looking sharp in lederhosen and a green felt hat with a white feather. He was pretending to choose an apple from a crate. The governess entered from stage left, clutching her basket. He smiled at her as she passed by, offering her an apple. Without warning, she reached into her basket, removed a short, thick club, and walloped him across the cranium.

"UUUUNNNNNHH!!!"

Roger winked at Debbie as he fell, but no one probably noticed, she thought.

On cue, she stood up and began clapping. Audience members on both sides of her looked at Debbie oddly, but a couple of them stood up and applauded, too. Then she could hear the rustling from one end of the auditorium to the other as people rose and knocked their hands together. The governess lost her usual menacing look, transformed into a confused bank teller again. The recently deceased Roger peeked at Debbie and his lifeless thumb ever so slightly pointed skyward, then he played dead again.

At the height of the applause, Debbie turned sharply and went up the aisle at a brisk pace, the ovation ebbing as she hit the exit. The door clunked shut behind her. She paused, looked at her timepiece again: 8:57. I'm not going to make it, she thought, running out to her bike. She quickly unlocked it and hopped on, pounding the pedals, heading for Main Street.

When she reached the Herald office, it was 9:08 and Griff Grimes was fiddling with his keys at the door.

"Mr. . . . Mr. Grimes!" she huffed, pulling up to the curb.

The editor turned, then glanced up and down the sidewalk before regarding her carefully and saying, "I was about to say I was afraid I scared you off, but I forgot who I was talking to."

"I'm sorry I'm late," she said. "I forgot I had a musical to go to."

"How was it?"

"Well, my boyfriend got a standing ovation."

"Good for him."

Climbing off the bicycle, she said, "Can I leave my bike here?"

"Let's put it in my car," Griff said, opening the trunk and setting it inside.

"Do I need to bring anything?" she asked.

"To the Cities?" He laughed. "No, you don't need to bring anything."

"Okay," she said with a grin, bouncing up and down on the pavement. "Let's go!"

"You know, Debster," Griff said, opening the car door for her, "you don't have anything to prove to me, or to anybody in town for that matter." She climbed into the car. "And as far as that old pageant goes, let me tell you that no one will remember or even care who was Scream Queen five, ten years down the road. The things you think are important now won't seem like much when you get older. Believe me, I've been there. Why don't I take you home?"

"Down the road," Debbie said softly, gazing off into some unimaginable distance. "Let's go."

11

The newspaper editor and his protégé drove for an hour in silence as the night settled in, leaving the cornfields and pastures of Atlantis County for the Dander River Valley and the towns of Katoville and St. CanDo. Debbie sat hunched forward, soaking up the road ahead, wondering what they might find around the next curve.

As they passed through Katoville, a small college town ringed by river bluffs, now dotted with clusters of lights, Debbie said, "I was here once for a Flag Day recital with my junior high choir. They fed us pizza burgers for dinner and I got sick."

"I graduated from Katoville State," Griff said. "Way back when."

"Oh, it couldn't have been that long ago."

"Much obliged."

"What was your major?"

He looked at her painfully. "Am I that lousy a newspaperman?"

"Well, you really should learn shorthand."

"You should learn your manners."

"Maybe so. I'm just feeling good. There's always so much pressure when Serial Killer Days comes around. The whole year gets shoved into one week, or that's the way it seems anyways. It feels good to get away from all that for a while."

"You know," Griff said, "we could just drive up the road a ways and turn around and head home. We could even go all the way to Sockton. They have a big billboard there advertising the Cities.

It has blinking lights and everything. We could just go that far . . ."

"How long before we get to the Cities?"

"Another hour and a half," he said.

Some time later they climbed out of the valley and came to Sockton, passing by the billboard without comment. Soon the skyline of the Cities could be seen: spires and lights and possibilities.

"Wow," Debbie said breathlessly. "It's so beautiful."

"From here it's a jewel," Griff said. "From here."

As they left Sockton they came to a cloverleaf leading onto a ten-lane highway, even at this late hour packed with cars whizzing along. "This is the final stretch," said Griff. "It's a straight shot into the Cities from here. It won't be long now. You'll get your wish."

"This is so great!" Debbie gushed.

The buildings, which had seemed toylike on the horizon not long ago, now grew taller and wider and Debbie was able to pick out details on some. She saw a skyscraper bathed in green light. A clock tower. A cathedral. One building looked like a blue crystal she had grown from a kit she had gotten for Christmas. But before long even those details were lost, looming out of sight above the car as they slowed into the center of the big city.

There didn't seem to be much activity on the streets. No one riding their bike or walking their dog. Taxi cabs zipped past them. The streets belonged to the cars, so that meant that all the activity, the taffy pulls and so forth, must be taking place in the tall buildings. Up ahead she saw the base of the blue crystal.

"Let me out here," she said.

Griff glanced at her. "I'm not going to let you out here. I'm not going to let you out of my sight."

"But you promised."

"All I said is that we'd be on the streets of the Cities at three in the morning. We can find an underage bar and listen to some music until then. Get something to eat. Anything you want."

"I want to get out here."

"Forget it."

"You said I was an adult, didn't you? You really can't tell me what to do, you know."

"You've seen the Cities now. There's really nothing else to show you. It's not all it's cracked up to be. Why don't we head home?"

The car stopped at a red light. Debbie opened her door. "Pick me up right here in a couple of hours," she said. Griff grabbed her wrist, but she broke free and hopped out of the car.

"Get back in here!" he yelled.

"I'll be okay, Mr. Grimes," she said with a confident smile, belying the way she felt inside. "Meet me here at . . ." She checked her watch. "Two A.M. Okay?"

The light changed. Cars began honking. "Wait here," he said. "There's a meter up ahead. Don't go anywhere." As he swung the car out of traffic and into the parking spot, Debbie flew off in the opposite direction, dodging cars as she cut across the street. She began running, up one street and down the next, until she was certain she had lost him.

Debbie felt happy as she skipped down the dirty street. She felt so free. Standard Springs never felt so far away. But she reminded herself that she was on a mission. *I may not have the throat muscles or the scars like the other girls, but here I am in the Cities while they are all at home sleeping away in their black bedrooms. They're just pretending, and though some may be able to pretend better than others, the judges, the whole town will look into my eyes and know that my fear is for real.*

But where should I start looking? Debbie wondered. *Is fear some unexpected, out-of-the-blue thing or is there a certain place, a certain time to find it? What would it be? A cab driver speaking rudely? Stepping in a puddle and having to ride all the way back home with wet shoes? Getting chased by a stray dog? Who the heck knew?*

Debbie walked along for a while and then she saw a barefoot man with torn clothes crawling into a big cardboard box on the sidewalk. She went up to his house and knocked, but nobody came to the door, so she said, "You know, sir, I've certainly seen odder houses in my life. Back in Standard Springs, that's my home town, ol' Lucky Pete lived in a thirty-gallon storage drum down by the old railroad station. There was also a friendly gal, I don't know her name, who resided in one of those big concrete ring deals they left behind after they built the highway."

Debbie leaned closer to the dark opening. "If I may be so bold, sir, I would suggest that you put your name and a street number on the outside of the box so you can get your mail and so people know where to visit you. That's what Lucky Pete did. He used to sing me songs when I was a kid, oh all sorts of songs like 'My Darling Clementine' and 'The Erie Canal,' he had a broken ukelele he'd strum. I'd sing with him, although I didn't know all the words."

She rested her arms on top of the box, her cheek brushing the cool cardboard surface. "I've never been to the Cities before, can you believe that? In fact, you're the first person I've met since I got here. It seems like a very nice place, although the buildings are bigger than the ones I'm used to back home. I'm a little worried I might get lost, too. I'm not going to be here very long, just a few hours, I have a ride that'll be waiting for me at the blue crystal building. It's a very lovely building, don't you think? I suppose you see it every day so it probably doesn't look like anything special to you, but it is very beautiful."

Sitting down on the pavement, Debbie tugged off her sneakers and left them at the entrance to the box. Barefoot, she continued down the street.

A man in the shadows of a building said something which she didn't fully understand, but she didn't feel like she could spare the time to ask for a clarification. After all, she only had two hours, less now, before she had to return home. She kept walking. The footsteps behind her, tapping on the sidewalk, comforted her. At least I'm not the only one out and about tonight, she thought.

Up ahead she saw a red neon sign outside an opaque storefront that said, THE FALLEN IDLE. As good a place as any to start, she thought, and went inside.

The interior was dark and a little smoky, light coming from candles in red glasses on the tables. Patrons, dressed mostly in black, were hunched over their tables, talking animatedly. There was a small stage at the far end of the room. A disheveled man wearing sunglasses and a leather jacket was mumbling into a microphone.

Debbie found a table next to a pillar haphazardly plastered with leaflets. She self-consciously settled into her seat. A dark-eyed girl wearing a black turtleneck and a silver earring in her nose came to the table. "Get you something?"

Smiling at her, Debbie said, "A glass of Florida sunshine would hit the spot right about now."

"Orange juice?"

"You betcha."

"Anything in it?"

"A straw would be nice."

The waitress disappeared.

Debbie turned her attention to the man on the stage. She could hear him better from here, although she wasn't exactly sure she understood his words.

". . . Idols burning, a fire, fire, like fires on fire, burn up the land, burn up the sea, you bourgeois swine."

Swine, Debbie thought, smiling.

The man sighed, took a drag on his cigarette, and shambled off the stage. Debbie clapped, shrinking into her chair when she saw that the people at nearby tables were giving her hostile looks.

A sullen woman in a wrinkled white dress shirt and purple spiked hair took his place on stage.

"Hang me now, oh world of tears, oh terrible tragedies, my life oh give it away to the angels of doom . . ."

The waitress returned with her juice. "Pardon me," said Debbie, "can just anybody get up on stage and start talking?"

"Sure, if the spirit moves you."

After the woman finished, Debbie stopped sitting on her hands and hopped up on stage. She gulped nervously, as conversations throughout the room broke off and heads turned to her.

"Sis boom bah!" someone called out mockingly.

"Hey," she said, "don't put down cheerleaders! They're as important as any of you out there! What kind of spirit would there be in the world without cheerleaders, for goodness sake?"

"Give us a cheer!" the same heckler shouted.

The patrons began laughing, quiet cool laughter, the candlelight reflecting off their shades.

Debbie lowered her head, tightly clutching the microphone, her knuckles blotching red and white, her long blonde hair hanging over her face.

Then she suddenly raised her head and opened her blue eyes wide.

"Once, if I recollect right, my life was a Sunday dinner with all the fixins, where every heart said howdy, where every brewski flowed!

"One night I gave Beauty a big ol' hug—and she didn't feel too swell, and I called her some sort of four-letter word. My hope has shriveled up like a prune. With a hop like a tomcat, I have caught and strangled every joy!"

"Go, baby, go!" someone yelled.

"I will tear the curtains from every mystery—mysteries of religion or hog farmin' or what have you. . . ."

She finished the poem, then retreated to the safety of the table, the patrons gazing at her but saying nothing. Debbie sipped her juice, keeping her eyes down. Gosh, I hope they're not mad at me, she thought. I'm a stranger here. I hope nobody yells at me or anything.

A few moments later a shadow fell over the table.

"That was wild," said a husky voice. "You're some poet."

Debbie slowly lifted her eyes. A somewhat overweight man in a goatee and beads stood above her, eyes hidden by narrow sunglasses. He had a tattoo of a strip of highway winding down his arm.

"Thanks," she said, "but it's not mine. That was one of Ole Rimbaud's new poems. He's the world greatest poet. I haven't read all the poets, but of the ones I have read he is definitely my favorite."

"Haven't heard of him. He lives in France?"

"Oh no, he's from Paristown, down in the southern part of the state. That's where I'm from, too. Standard Springs, to be exact."

The man looked over his shoulder and whistled. Four or five folks came over and gathered around her table.

"Chick says the dude who wrote it is Ole Rimbaud," the goatee man told his cohorts. "Anybody know him?"

Shrugs and negatives all around.

"He keeps a pretty low profile," Debbie explained. "He's got a hog farm to take care of, which probably keeps his hands full."

"We should get him to contribute to *Give Up!,*" said a red-haired woman in a beret next to the goatee man. "Do you know where we can get hold of him?"

"Well, the address on the books is a post office box in Paristown. Barrow Publishing. It's not that big a town. It's right off Highway Ninety-nine, the Arrow Highway, it's called."

"Cool."

"Hey," said the man with the goatee, "do you want to come back to our pad and groove? It's just down the street."

"Sure," Debbie said. "I'd like that."

"My name's Jim Bowie. This is Latisha, Zipper, Roc, Lazy Larry."

"Hi, everybody. I'm Debbie Sue Morning."

So the group paid up their tabs and left the Fallen Idle. They headed down the sidewalk, Debbie in the middle, feeling a bit high from her juice. She looked up at the skyscrapers, craning her neck so far that she almost stumbled over backward. The woman with the beret, Latisha, looped a supporting arm around her shoulder.

"We don't have buildings like this back home," Debbie said with an embarrassed grin.

"A real small-town girl, aren't you?"

"I guess I am."

"Don't get caught up in buildings that scrape the stars from the sky, don't give your life to the ones who cannot cry."

"That's a nice poem. Who wrote it?"

"I did."

"Wow!"

"We're all poets," said Jim Bowie, as they came to an old brick building with a pawn shop at street level. They climbed the dark, musty stairs and went down to the end of the short hallway. A moth did frantic loops around a fluorescent light overhead. Poor guy, Debbie thought.

"Home is where the poem is," Jim Bowie said, opening the door and ushering everyone inside with a grand, sweeping gesture. The lights came on, and Debbie looked around. The room was cluttered with books, papers, psychedelic posters, and lava lamps. "Sorry, the house cleaner had the week off," explained Jim Bowie, and everyone laughed. He grabbed a stack of magazines from a shelf while his comrades sat in a circle on the scuffed wooden floor.

"Here's our pride and sorrow," Bowie said, handing the pile of publications to Debbie. She took the top one. GIVE UP!, it said in big block letters at the top. There was a picture of a noose on the cover. Inside the noose was a smiley face. Flipping to the contents page, she recognized some of their names. One poem was called "Oblong Misery" by Latisha Swea. Debbie turned to that page.

"The dead don't breathe or eat or drink or dream / we are alive / but we don't live / oh oblong box / oh oblong misery . . ."

"Hey, this is like Ole Rimbaud's poems," Debbie said. "I like it, Latisha."

"Thanks," she said. "Do you ever write poems?"

"No, I've never written even one. I'm pretty happy, actually."

"Really."

"Is it okay that I'm not afraid?"

Latisha smiled. "Of course. We're not afraid, are we, Jim Bowie?"

"We are fearless and desolate and shining," said their leader.

"Fearless," Debbie repeated dreamily.

"Yeah," Latisha said.

"I thought everybody would be afraid in the Cities," Debbie said. "Isn't everybody afraid everywhere? That's the way it seems to me. I do want to get along with people, though, you know, feel like we have something in common, something to bind us together; you really need that to live, don't you?"

"Sure," agreed Latisha.

"I don't particularly *want* to be afraid," Debbie continued. "But I'm learning, I'm working on my fears. I'm certainly much more afraid than I was last year."

"You don't *look* all that afraid," said Lazy Larry, a curly-haired fellow wearing a fringed vest.

"Well I am! Ask anyone who knows me."

"If you say so."

"My teacher told me I had nothing to fear but fear itself," Debbie said. "I thought that was a neat thing to say."

"Wild," someone said.

"It's different living in a small town," Debbie said. "We don't have anything like the Fallen Idle; oh, the Legion is pretty nice, especially when they have a taco feed, but you might get a funny look if you got up and started reading poetry, unless it was Mother Goose or something. I mean, nobody's hardly heard of Ole Rimbaud, for goodness sake, and the people that have don't understand him. I mean, he'd probably be normal, even honored, if he lived in the Cities. He loves his hogs, but gosh, a person needs some appreciation once in a while, too."

"Are you really a cheerleader?" Latisha asked.

"Sure am! I'm a football cheer squad member, to be exact."

"I was the one who ragged on you at the Idle," Lazy Larry said. "I was out of line. I'm sorry."

"It's okay. But, you know, football is a wonderful sport. Why, one time last season, I think we were playing Nodal High, a squirrel got loose on the field and the referees chased it all over the place and one of them tripped and fell in the mud! Boy, we sure laughed hard at that one. He wasn't hurt or anything; his uniform just got all dirty and he couldn't change clothes until after the game."

"I used to play football," Jim Bowie admitted.

"Wow, Jim, really?" Zipper asked.

"It's true," he said. "I played up until my junior year in high school. One day coach has us doing wind sprints, run until you see black, he says. Well, I saw black and walked off the field and I've been seeing black ever since. Thank you, coach."

"Give us a cheer," Latisha prompted Debbie, smiling.

"Sure!" Debbie said, jumping to her feet. "Okay, so like pretend the other team is marching down to our end of the field and is about to score, and we turn to our crowd and say . . ." she clenched her fists and held them high, "be like iron, be like steel, to our greatness you will kneel!" Now her hands, which had saluted the floor at the word "kneel," moved above her head again and flapped like flags in a windstorm. "DEE-FENSE! DEE-FENSE!" she shouted, faster and faster. "DEFENSE! DEFENSE! DEFENSE!" Faster and faster still. "DEFENSE! DEFENSE! DEFENSE! DEFENSE! DEFENSE!" Finally, Debbie spun around and collapsed breathlessly to the floor, a happy look on her face.

The Idlers whooped in appreciation.

"Whoa," said Debbie, weaving as she sat up. "I do believe I'm just a little bit out of practice."

"You are one wild cheerleading angel," Jim Bowie said.

The gang talked on about things great and dangerous, read poetry, sipped tea, and practiced cheers. Some time later Debbie glanced at her watch. It was 1:45. "Oh my gosh!" she exclaimed, popping up. "I've got to run. Someone's meeting me at two and I've still got an errand to do."

"What a drag," said Jim Bowie.

"Yeah, man," Latisha said. "We were grooving on you."

"I was having fun, too. Maybe I can come back some day and visit you all again."

"Take one of our magazines," Jim told her, with a touch of emotion in his eyes, handing her the copy of *Give Up!* featuring the hanging smiley. "Write us or contribute a poem or just read it and remember us."

"Thanks," Debbie said.

Giving her a hug, Latisha whispered in her ear, "Be like iron, be like steel, okay?"

"I'll be all right. You take care, too, Latisha."

Debbie left the Idlers, going down the hallway, down the stairs, the floor cold on her bare feet. At the base of the stairway, she pushed open the door, and found herself on the pavement, alone. Where's the blue crystal from here? she wondered, stepping into the street, scanning the sky as she turned a circle. She walked down a block, back up toward the bar, then turned the corner and saw the peak of the crystal, a blue beacon illuminating the city sky.

Feeling better at having found this familiar landmark, Debbie set off for her rendezvous. As Debbie hurried along, she chided herself for having spent most of her time in the city having fun instead of completing her chore. I can't forget the whole reason why I dared to come here, she thought. I may be a long way from home, but I still have to keep up my concentration.

As she neared the blue tower, Debbie peered down the dark alleyways, looking for a likely prospect. She spotted a few folks lifting paper sacks to their mouths, a stray cat, a rat. Finally, as she came to the intersection where the blue skyscraper was located, she saw Mr. Grimes pacing nervously outside his car, which was parked at the curb. Stopping, she spotted a burly man standing near a pair of green Dumpsters not far away. The man was staring at her. She quickly approached him. "Say, have you got change for a hundred?" she cheerily asked.

The stranger took a step toward her. "Sure, honey," he said, an odd look in his eyes. She retreated a pace, another, then he pulled a short pipe from his jacket and swung at her. Debbie ducked enough so that the blow struck her on the top left of her forehead. It hurt quite a bit, and she dropped her magazine, but she stayed on her feet, pretending to be on the verge of collapse, and as he raised the pipe again, she darted away. As Debbie ran toward the intersection, she glanced back and saw that the attacker had pulled up.

Fingering the lump on her head, feeling the wetness on her fingers, she hurried to Griff's car.

"Hi!" she said, coming up behind him.

He whirled, an explosion of relief and concern on his face quickly muted. "It's about time you showed up," he said, inspecting her wound. "I was about to leave without you. It's a long walk back to Standard Springs."

"Thanks for waiting. Let's go home, huh?"

He glanced down. "Lose your shoes?"

"I like going barefoot," she said.

They climbed into the car. Griff gave her a handkerchief to stop the bleeding. They pulled into traffic and soon were on the big highway heading out of the Cities. Debbie propped her feet on the dashboard and hummed along to the drumming of the tires on the dark road.

12

Standard Springs appeared different somehow to Debbie as Griff Grimes took the exit off the highway and tooled by the junkyard toward the center of town. She wasn't sure if this was because she had never before seen her town at four-thirty in the morning, or if something inside her had changed. It was late. Or early. Riding with the window down, her head resting on her arms draped onto the window frame, gazing at the dark town, Debbie could hear the first birds of morning already cooing and singing. The excitement was draining away, and she was beginning to feel quite tired.

As they came to her house, Griff said, "You should get that cut looked at. First thing."

"It's just a little bump," said Debbie.

"What are you going to tell your parents?"

She shrugged. "I'll think of something."

He let her off outside the gate, taking her bicycle out of the trunk.

"Thanks, Mr. Grimes," she said.

"See you later, kid."

Debbie walked her bike around the house to the back door, leaving it by the step, then went inside. It was quiet, the ticking of the kitchen clock tracking her footsteps. Thankfully there were no early risers. Debbie climbed the stairs and went into her room, latching the door behind her. Washing her face, she winced, feeling the sting of water on her wound. Looking in the mirror, she was pleased to see that the gash, even after getting the dried blood washed from it, still retained an impressive patina.

Debbie set her alarm and crawled into bed, pulling the sheet up to her neck. She felt exhausted, but her mind kept whirring. Did I accomplish what I set out to do? she wondered. The wound obviously improved her chances of success at the pageant, but had she brought anything back from the Cities other than this superficial emblem? Hmm, she thought, that's a good question. Do I feel the fear inside any more than I did yesterday? It's hard to say. I don't think I do, but maybe it's one of those things that comes on gradually, that you don't really notice until one day you wake up and find yourself too frightened to leave the house. Well, she concluded, at the worst I've got a nice wound and hopefully Miss Exeter will notice and maybe even Samantha and the other contestants will like me again. . . .

●

Not more than ten minutes later, or so it seemed to Debbie, the alarm clock buzzed. She forced herself out of bed, got dressed quickly, and headed downstairs. Her mother was in the kitchen, watering the plants on the window sill above the sink.

"Morning, Mom," Debbie said with a trace of anxiety.

"Morning, dear. I didn't expect you up until noon."

"I came back from Miss Exeter's a little earlier than I expected, so I could get some extra sleep. I'm helping out with the tours today. Have to be down at the Chamber of Commerce by nine to pick up my uniform."

"I hope you didn't forget that you promised to take Bobby to the midway tonight."

"No, Mom, I didn't forget."

"How was the party?"

"It was fun. A lot of fun."

"Maybe a little too much fun," her mother said, coming over and inspecting her wound.

"It's no big deal, Mom. We were playing Ping-Pong and I

slipped and hit my head on the edge of the table. It hurt for a while, but I'm okay now."

"We should put a dressing on it, dear."

"It should get air. That's what Miss Exeter said. She's trained in first aid, you know."

A worried expression still on her face, her mother said, "I hope it doesn't get infected."

Hey, *infection,* Debbie thought.

"When do you think you'll be back?" Mother asked.

"Probably by lunchtime. I'll be able to sleep the rest of the afternoon and be fresh to take Bobby tonight." She downed a half glass of orange juice and kissed her mom on the cheek. "Gotta run. Say hi to Dad for me. And tell Bobby to get ready for those rides."

"Have a nice time, dear."

Debbie went out through the kitchen, taking a deep breath as the screen door slammed behind her. Boy, I'm getting pretty good at this lying business, she thought. Well, it would be much worse for Mom to know what really happened. It's for her own protection, for goodness sake. Hopping on her bike, Debbie pedaled around the house and coasted down the driveway, feeling the cool morning breeze sweep her hair and face, her lie receding in the distance, and she thought that perhaps this might be a good day after all.

When she reached the Chamber of Commerce office, located one block south of Main Street, Debbie jumped off her bike, leaning it beside the door, and went inside.

"Hi, Weddy," Debbie said to the small silver-haired woman at the desk, wearing a Serial Killer Days T-shirt.

"Good morning, Debra," said the stone-faced chamber prez. "Are you ready for the grand tour?"

"You bet!"

Going over to a closet on the wall, Weddy removed some garments and said, "Here you go."

Debbie took the black jacket with a badge on the shoulder bearing the initials *SKD* and the conductor-style cap with a similar insignia. She slipped into the jacket; it was still a little big, though not as roomy as last year. The hat fit fine. "I guess I'm set, then," she said.

"Don't get in a wreck," said Weddy, giving her a key ring. "And remember," she poked her index fingers at the corners of her mouth, "no smiling!"

Debbie rode her bike the short distance to Kraven Park, noticing as she approached that a sizable crowd had already gathered around the natural gas trolley car in the parking lot. Older tourists in straw hats, cameras looped around their necks. Kids with antsy mothers. A teenage couple holding hands. She locked up her bike and hopped into the front of the vehicle, announcing, "All aboard, folks! We'll be leaving in a couple of minutes, so make yourselves comfortable and get ready to enjoy the one and only Serial Killer Days' Tour of Fear." The assemblage piled on eagerly, Debbie gathering their tickets, then they watched her attentively for further instructions. "The tour will last approximately one hour," Debbie continued. "Please feel free to ask questions at any time as we visit the various historic sites. Please do not stand up or attempt to leave the trolley while it is moving. My name is Debbie, by the by. Are there any questions before we get started?"

A white-haired gentleman in a purple muscle shirt and plaid hiking shorts raised his hand high.

"Sir?"

"Will there be any dead bodies or blood or anything? My bride here is a little nervous, but I told her she could close her eyes when we get to the icky parts."

The woman whacked him on the arm, frowning.

"This is an educational tour, sir," Debbie said. "Although some of the descriptions may be graphic, there will be no unnecessary displays of violence."

A couple of disappointed groans came from the ranks of the passengers.

"However, if you look closely at some of our stops you may be able to spot some *dried* blood. You just can't get out those pesky blood stains, as I'm sure many of our mothers with us today know."

Feminine laughter rippled through the car.

Debbie sat down in the driver's seat. After starting up the trolley car, she unwound the microphone cord and glanced in the rearview mirror to make sure everyone was seated. Then she pulled out of the parking lot, steering with her left hand, holding the squat gray microphone to her mouth.

"Our first stop will be at the site of our serial killer's very first attack, some twenty-one years ago," Debbie recited in a monotone. She turned the corner and drove down Dew Line Lane, stopping outside a two-story white house with meticulously trimmed grass and a bronze plaque on a pole at the bottom of the steps.

"This used to be the Crawmeyer residence," Debbie told the passengers. "Mr. Crawmeyer owned the furniture store downtown for many years. He was on the county board for a while, too. Now if you look at the first-story window on the left side of the house, the main bedroom, that's where the serial killer entered the residence and killed Mrs. Crawmeyer."

Cameras clicked.

"Do they still live there?" a man asked.

"Mr. Crawmeyer and his two daughters moved out of the house about a year after the attack. They lived on the north end of town until his daughters graduated, then he left town for good. Not sure where he ended up. The city bought the house seven years ago as a historic site and has maintained it since then."

"What kind of weapon did he use?" someone inquired.

"Police believed it was a hatchet," Debbie responded, "although no weapon was ever found."

Debbie let them finish taking their snapshots, then proceeded to the next site, located three blocks up the street. The old Aztec-styled Victorian house was straddled by a wooded area. There were faded red x's beneath all the windows and on the front door.

"This is a very important house," explained Debbie. Cameras snapped. "This marked the first time that the now familiar red x's were used by families who were victimized once and did not want to be attacked again. After the serial killer murdered their daughter, Joe and Jane Plenty mistakenly thought that lightning couldn't strike twice. Unfortunately, the Plentys lost another daughter the very next year, the first and only time a household was victimized twice in consecutive years."

The passengers gave a sympathetic groan.

"Mrs. Plenty responded by purchasing a bucket of red paint and marking the house as seen here. Her strategy was successful, and the Plentys have lived worry-free in the years since. Their practice has caught on and is now the traditional response by the family of each year's victim."

"See, I told you it wasn't just a lousy paint job," someone commented.

"Looks like there's a pattern to these killings," said a gravelly voice. "Is there a pattern here?"

"You're welcome to find one, sir," Debbie said, "although I must say that the best law enforcement minds of Standard Springs have been trying to discover one for many years without luck."

"Looks like a pattern to me," the same man mumbled.

Driving to the next stop, Debbie's mind began to wander as the familiar patter tumbled out of her mouth without her even thinking about it. She felt a warmness in her heart as she thought about her time with the Idle gang in the Cities. It was hard to imagine she was with them only a few hours ago; it seemed like another lifetime, or a dream. There can't really be people in the world like Jim Bowie and his friends, she thought. Maybe the honey is still messing up my brain.

". . . one of the odder cases. After the serial killer attacked Mrs. Google, her husband suffered a heart attack and died. Although the killer did not place a finger on Mr. Google, he could, if ever caught, be charged with both murders."

"I didn't know that!" someone exclaimed.

"Why can't they catch him?" a little boy asked.

"Now don't bother the nice lady," said a doting voice.

"I don't mind answering him, ma'am." Debbie glanced back at the boy. "What's your name?"

"Tommy."

"Do you have a piggy bank, Tommy?"

"Sure! It's almost full!"

"How many pennies are in it?"

"Five hundred and twelve!"

"So imagine if you had nine or ten piggy banks like that and you broke them and put all the pennies in a big pile and then picked just one penny out of all those pennies."

"Ten piggy banks!" Tommy said happily.

"So you put all the pennies in a big pile and . . ."

"Ten piggy banks," repeated Tommy, giggling, sliding down in his seat.

Debbie watched him until he disappeared, then said slowly, "Okay, well, from here we'll be heading uptown to take a short break. You can grab a cup of coffee and a donut at Weed's Bakery, or buy a button or toy knife or one of the other wide selection of souvenirs available at the Official Serial Killer Days' Booster Shop, major credit cards accepted."

They puttered into the downtown area, Debbie pulling to the curb outside the souvenir shop. She spotted her dad coming out of the bakery, stuffing a pastry into his mouth with one hand, carrying a sheaf of papers in the other, trying to read between bites. "Fifteen minutes on our stop," she told the passengers, and stepped down to the pavement as the tourists disembarked.

"Hey, Dad!" she called out, running down the sidewalk. "Wait up!"

Mr. Morning turned back, squeezing out a fatherly grin from his tension-wracked face. "Say, you certainly look sharp today. How's the tour going?"

"Okay, I guess. How's the parade looking?"

"Everything's under control, for now. But it's only nine-thirty."

She tipped back her hat without thinking, wiping the sweat from her brow, feeling the scabby ridge.

"My gosh," said her father, "that's a nasty gouge you've got there. What happened?"

"It's okay, Dad. I just tripped and fell at the slumber party last night." She pulled her hat down again. "Say, what has to happen for a wound to get infected?"

"Well, sweetheart, I'm no doctor, but I would say that not washing it is probably the main cause."

Debbie made a mental note.

"All ready for the big pageant?" her father asked.

"I guess I am. It's hard to believe it's my last one. I guess I'm getting old, huh."

"You're still five years old to me. Always have been."

"Say, Dad, did Mom talk to you about Bobby going with me and Roger to the midway tonight?"

"I believe she did mention it, although I can't recall exactly what she said about it."

"Well, do you want us to let Bobby go on all the rides? He wants to, but he's pretty young for some of them."

"Oh, absolutely. He's sure not ready for the Open Bedroom Window or the Parking Ramp at Midnight. He'll have fun in Kiddieland. I think the Scary-Go-Round will be more than enough for someone his age."

"How about the Dark Pond?"

"I think he could handle that."

Debbie glanced back at the trolley. Some of the passengers were climbing back on. "I'd better get going, Dad. I'll see you later. Are you going to be home for dinner?"

"Doubtful. Have a good time tonight."

"Bye!"

Debbie headed back to the tour bus in a fine mood after basking in her dad's attention. But to her dismay she found a parking ticket on the windshield. Boy, that was quick work, she thought. After waiting a couple of minutes she did a head count, then started up the trolley and turned onto Bludgeon Street.

"Bludgeon Street takes its name from the attack that occurred in the blue house up ahead some five years ago . . ."

13

Deputy Dan felt their eyes boring into him. His heart hammered. His lips grew dry. He shifted from foot to foot, looking down, then he slowly, painfully lifted his head and gazed at those who tormented him.

"Are you okay, mister?" asked a freckled youngster in a cub scout uniform on his knees, pulling himself across the gymnasium floor to the feet of the Deputy. Motioning the boy away, Deputy Dan licked his lips and said, his voice breaking, "Welcome, today, children. Thank you for volunteering to participate in the Serial Killer Days' Parking Control Program. I notice that there are fewer of you in attendance today than last year, and while it's sad to witness the decline of volunteerism in our community . . ."

"Jessie Escher moved *away*," a brownie with pigtails said knowingly, rolling her eyes.

". . . uh, all you young people here today should be saluted." Deputy Dan self-consciously saluted them. Many of the cub scouts returned the gesture, including some who hit nearby scouts on the head and arm at the tail end of their salutes.

"Your job will consist of two parts," said the Deputy, raising two fingers above his head. "Part One is parking control. Parking control involves ensuring that the public parks their cars in an orderly manner. You will learn the proper use of traffic cones, hand signals, including left, right, and stop (the Deputy demonstrated these as he spoke), and what to do in case of a parking-related disaster or other emergency. Part Two is being an ambassador for Serial Killer Days."

"What kind of door is that?" a cub scout asked, receiving several slugs on the arm for his effort.

"As an ambassador for Serial Killer Days, your responsibility is to treat our visitors in a friendly, courteous manner. If they have any questions, do your best to answer them. Always remember that they are our guests. Always remember . . ."

"I'm gonna be a Webelo," said a young man. "We all blow!" He threw his head back and blew out air, then slugged a neighbor on the shoulder.

Deputy Dan began to worry as he concluded his remarks to the scouts. How am I ever going to be able to confront the Sheriff if I can hardly look these kids in the eye? Have to work my courage up.

Kids, did you know that at this very minute the serial killer is sitting in our jailhouse?

"When you have completed your duties, as a reward for all your help each of you will receive an official Serial Killer Days' baseball cap and a certificate of recognition." The Deputy held up a cap and brandished it in front of the boys and girls, who made noises indicating their approval.

An hour later, Deputy Dan gathered up his practice traffic cones and said, "Thank you very much for attending this training session. Don't forget to report back here on Saturday at ten P.M. sharp. If you can't make it for some reason, just call or stop in at the Sheriff's office. Are there any questions?"

A brownie down by his left shoe timidly poked her hand up. The Deputy nodded at her. "Yes?"

"I can see up your nose," she said shyly.

●

Driving back uptown, Deputy Dan spotted the Serial Killer Days trolley car parked illegally in front of a fire hydrant right outside the souvenir shop. The trolley was empty. What if a fire suddenly broke out at the bakery? he thought with indignation. He pulled up alongside the trolley, scribbled out a ticket and left it under the windshield wiper.

Deputy Dan drove back to the jailhouse, still feeling a little steamed. A very poor example to set for our visitors, he thought. People will think we're a bunch of law-breaking hooligans. He parked outside the Sheriff's office and went to the entrance. Pulling open the door, he heard voices coming from inside. Unfamiliar voices, and rather loud. He entered the room, one hand on his service revolver. As his eyes adjusted to the light, he still heard the voices, but the place was empty, apart from the prisoner.

"What the . . ." said the Deputy, slowly walking over to the cell. The prisoner was watching television. There was a television, color no less, inside the prisoner's cell. A *television*. He lay on his cot, a big pillow behind his head. He was wearing sunglasses, the sun blazing in from the high cell window. There was the smell of suntan lotion in the room. The Deputy watched the strange scene in confusion. Things weren't like this when I left this morning, he said to himself. I know they weren't. The prisoner began chuckling at something he saw on the illegal television.

"Hey, you! What's going on here?" Deputy Dan asked him, briskly striding to the cell.

The prisoner glanced over and gave him a languid wave. "Hiya, Deputy. How's the criminal world treating you today?"

"What's going on here?" the Deputy repeated. "You can't have a television."

"I can't?"

"Of course you can't. It's against the rules."

"Well, I didn't know that."

"No prisoner has *ever* got their own TV," said the Deputy.

"How am I supposed to know that? I just got here." The man took a brown bottle from the floor and raised it to his lips.

"Is that *beer?*" Deputy Dan asked.

"It's not just beer, it's Squirrel's Eye Beer. Brewed from fresh spring water."

"You're in big trouble!" the Deputy said. He tried to unlock the cell, finding unexpectedly that it was not locked at all. "Party time's over!" he said, yanking out the cord to the television and lifting it off the table.

"Hey, I was watching that!" the prisoner protested.

"Deputy! What in all blue heck do you think you're doing?" came a booming voice from outside the cell.

Startled, Deputy Dan dropped the television. It made a loud thud when it hit the floor. Sheriff Eeha entered the cell with a worried look on his face. He put the television back on the table and plugged it in. The picture appeared twisted and snowy. "Now you've gone and done it," said the Sheriff angrily.

"Try the rabbit ears," the prisoner suggested.

"Good idea." Sheriff Eeha fiddled with the antenna, improving the picture somewhat, then said apologetically, "We'll get this fixed pronto, Mr. Centaur. Either that or a certain deputy will go buy you a new one out of his salary."

"Don't break a gut," the prisoner said with a generous wave of his hand. "I was getting tired of watching it, anyway. Hey, it'd sure be nice to have a pizza for lunch."

"No problem," said the Sheriff, closing the cell door behind himself and the Deputy. "What do you want on it?"

"The works."

"Anchovies?"

"Why not? And make sure there's bacon on it, okay? None of that Canadian crap, though."

"What would you like to drink?"

"Another beer would be nice. You know, it'd be swell to have a small refrigerator in here."

"I'll see what I can do."

"Much obliged."

Sheriff Eeha grabbed Deputy Dan by the elbow and led him to the back room, cluttered with file cabinets, yellowed wanted posters, and dusty bowling trophies. Shutting the door behind them, the Sheriff stuck his hands on his hips and said in a low voice, "Deputy, do you have any idea who that man is out there?"

"Uh, I think I do."

"Well, it's obvious you don't know or else you wouldn't have treated him like a common criminal."

"But I thought . . ."

The Sheriff pointed at the door. "That man is the star of the show, Deputy. Come Saturday night he is going to be riding high in a cage on top of the Scream Queen float. You can't get much more important than that." Sheriff Eeha removed his hat, holding it to his chest. "He is an honored guest, Deputy, and it is our duty to make him as comfortable as we can until Saturday night. An *honored guest,* Deputy. Do I make myself clear?"

"Yes, sir."

"Now I want you to coordinate the acquisition of the pizza. Remember what he said about the Canadian bacon. And *whatever* you do, don't forget the beer."

"Yes, sir."

As the Sheriff turned to leave, Deputy Dan said quietly, "Uh, Sheriff Eeha, there's something I have to tell you."

Turning back, Sheriff Eeha looked at his deputy expectantly. "Well, what is it?"

Gulping, Deputy Dan said, "Sir, I have reason to believe that the man out there, the, uh, prisoner, is, well, the man who's been doing all the killings, that he is . . . the killer."

Sheriff Eeha clapped the Deputy on the shoulder. "Now you're getting the hang of it, son!"

"I'm not pretending," said the Deputy, a trace of firmness in his voice.

The Sheriff got a funny look on his face. "What are you talking about, boy?"

The urge to epoxy his eyes to the floor surged through Deputy Dan, but he kept them level, focused on the Sheriff. "I have reason to believe that our prisoner out there is the serial killer who's been coming to our town every July for the past twenty-one years."

Sheriff Eeha said nothing for a minute, just stared at the Deputy, a slight tic on the left side of his mouth. His ears reddened. Finally, he said, slowly, "Do you have any evidence of this, Deputy?"

"It's like this, Sheriff. When I talked to Mrs. Flatwire, she said he told her that he came to town for Serial Killer Days. He's a loner, you can see it. He doesn't talk about himself. Is it just a coincidence that he came to town a few days before our annual killing?"

"Is that all you've got for proof?"

"Well, no. Junior Sasser showed me how to use a divining rod. You know, it can find things. You just think about it and the rod bends toward what you're looking for. I tried it on the prisoner the other night. It bent, so hard that it broke in two. I *don't* know for certain that it's him, but we sure can't take any chances, can we?"

The Sheriff said nothing.

"At least let's hold him through Saturday night. That way, if nobody gets killed then we'll know it's him. And if somebody *does* get killed, why then there's no harm done and we release him. It's just a matter of hanging onto him for a few hours more than we planned. Isn't that worth it, sir?"

Looking away, the Sheriff said softly, "Shouldn't you be getting the pizza, Deputy?"

"But . . ." the Deputy began, then hung his head and left the back room. As he was about to leave the jailhouse, Deputy Dan looked back and saw Sheriff Eeha at his desk, peering intently at a small notebook.

14

The trip to the fairgrounds on the east side of town, site of the midway, was just a few minutes in length, yet even that was an unbearably long ordeal for Bobby. He rode in the back with his head out the window the whole way, asking every block, "Are we there yet? Are we there yet?"

"Get your head back in the car," Debbie said, tugging at his T-shirt. "You don't want to swallow a bug, do you?"

Bobby opened his mouth wider.

Roger cackled. "I knew a guy once who stuck his head out the window like that and a car came truckin' around the corner and blammo!"

"You did not," said Debbie.

"Sure I did. Why would I make somethin' like that up?"

"Who was it?"

"A cousin of mine."

"A cousin, huh. What was his name?"

"My cousin Ben, Ben Dover," he said, paused, then fell into hysterics.

"Oh, *Roger,*" Debbie said.

At last they arrived at the fairgrounds. Roger wheeled his heap into the grassy parking area near the livestock barn. Even though there were no parking stripes or other indicators, all the cars were parked in an orderly manner. It was dark, and the lights of the midway were muted, although the illumination in Kiddieland was somewhat merrier. The whole midway seemed brighter than what Debbie remembered from her excursions as a youngster. She wasn't sure if it was the passage of time that made her memories darker or if the midway operators had softened over the years. Kids are so pampered these days, she thought.

The trio left the car and headed over to the ticket booth at the edge of the midway. A bare bulb in the peak of the shack flickered. Roger bought a string of orange tickets, and they hurried to keep up with Bobby as he hurtled into the heart of Kiddieland.

"What do you want to go on first?" Debbie asked, trying to snatch his hand.

"Scary-Go-Round! Scary-Go-Round!" shouted Bobby, racing over to the dark ride.

Debbie handed the sullen youth at the gate two tickets as Bobby scampered onto the ride. He weaved among the various creatures, most with open maw and claws displayed, finally settling atop a German Shepherd with a foaming mouth.

"Leave it to Bobby to pick a doggie," Debbie said.

The carousel began to rotate slowly, the smaller kids hanging on for their lives, the older ones hopping up and down and carrying on. Morbid synthesized music throbbed from a cheap speaker mounted on top of the ride. Debbie waved at Bobby every time he came around; he waved back each time, too, making a growling face, pretending the plastic hound was chomping on his hand.

"It was sweet of you to let Bobby come along with us," Debbie told Roger as her brother disappeared around the back stretch again. "It's all I've been hearing about for a week: 'When's Roger going to take us to the rides?' He really likes you, Rog."

"The kid kinda reminds me of myself when I was a little tyke. How have those dog pills been working out?"

"He seems to be a little more under control," Debbie said, waving, "although you can't tell it by the way he's acting tonight. Let me know if he starts getting on your nerves."

"Hey, you can't blame him for being excited. It is Serial Killer Days, after all."

Soon the carousel cruised to a stop and the music ended. Bobby hopped off the rabid dog and tore back to Debbie and Roger.

"Was it fun?" Debbie asked.

"I want to ride again!" Bobby said, popping up and down.

"Maybe later. How would you like some cotton candy?"

"Yeah! Candy!" Bobby shouted.

They went over to a nearby trailer that sold snacks. "Cotton candy, please," she told the woman at the window, handing her fifty cents. The woman spun the sugary black cotton onto a paper cone and gave it to Debbie. She tore off a bit before passing it to Bobby. She wasn't a big fan of black licorice, but the taste brought back pleasant memories. Bobby stuffed a big handful into his mouth, making his face all sticky.

"Slow down," Debbie chided. "We're going to be here all night, remember?"

Bobby grinned and this time used both hands to cram the candy into his mouth.

"Where next?" Debbie asked Roger.

"The Dark Pond is always fun."

Kneeling down, Debbie said, "Do you want to go to the Dark Pond, Bobby? Everybody wins a prize there."

"Prizes!" Bobby said.

"I'll take that as a yes," said Debbie, and so they headed off to the Dark Pond, located next door to the kiddie Ferris wheel. Debbie smiled when she saw the pond, which was actually a cardboard wall painted black with lily pads and froggies pasted onto the surface. A group of cane poles leaned up against the wall, clothespins attached to the lines.

Handing her ticket to the operator, Debbie told Bobby, "Now here's how you do it. Just pick any of the poles and throw your line over the wall, into the pond, see? Then when you feel a bite pull the line back over the wall and see what you caught."

"Oh boy!" Bobby said, running over to the wall and grabbing a pole. His first two casts were unsuccessful, the clothespin harmlessly thwacking the wall not much more than halfway up.

"Do you want me to help you?" Debbie asked.

"No!" Stepping back, his little jaw jutting out, Bobby drew the pole back, took a couple of quick hops, and whipped the pole forward, sending the clothespin sailing safely over the wall.

"Nice shot, kid," said Roger.

A few seconds later the line began jiggling.

"Look, Bobby, you've got a bite!" Debbie said.

"Looks like a whopper," said Roger.

Legs pumping, Bobby pulled the line back over to their side of the wall. Attached to the clothespin was Something Dripping.

At least they aren't giving away cheap prizes that will fall apart as soon as you get home, Debbie thought. She knew that Bobby had wanted one on his last birthday, but it had somehow slipped through the cracks amidst all the hoopla.

Wide-eyed Bobby waved his prize around in a frenzied fashion, spattering Debbie's clean white T-shirt.

"Now you be careful with that," she said, dabbing at the stain, which was already disappearing, "or we'll put it in the car and you'll have to wait until we get home to play with it."

Bobby settled down somewhat after her admonishment, and they strolled along, leaving Kiddieland and going into the carnival area of the midway. It was more crowded in this section, couples young and old holding hands, teenage boys strutting, clutching big pink monkeys and wolverines won at some test of strength or courage.

Suddenly, Debbie felt something heavy and alive land on her shoulder. She was too startled to scream. She quickly turned her head and found herself eye to eye with a real live monkey. It was a small spider monkey wearing a red hat and vest with gold buttons. It chattered at her.

Roger began laughing.

"Many apologies, madam," said a dark-haired man in a gypsy costume coming out from a nearby tent, his accent more Norwegian than Gypsy. He pulled the monkey from her shoulder. "Lucifer has been very naughty tonight. May I tell you your fortune in payment for your trouble, eh?"

"Really? I've never had my fortune told before."

"This way," he said, gesturing at his tent.

They went through the tent flaps, decorated with beads and colorful tapestries. A sign on the wall said UFF DA. Debbie sat down at his table, the centerpiece of which was a glowing crystal ball.

"Your friends must wait outside," said the gypsy, seating himself opposite Debbie, letting the monkey jump to the ground.

"It's okay, Rog," Debbie said. "I'll be right out."

"I'll win you a prize," Rog said, taking Bobby's hand. "Come on, half-pint, let's have some fun." They disappeared through the flaps.

The gypsy, Debbie noticed, seemed to be losing his sweeping black mustache. One end was drooping, a thread of glue being pulled down by the weight of the appliance. He didn't seem to notice or mind, and began rubbing the crystal ball. His blue eyes, weighed down by a set of bushy black eyebrows, didn't waver from her.

"Place your hands on the ball," he said, "and clear your mind."

Debbie tentatively moved her hands toward the ball, and touched it, feeling the warmth envelope her fingers. Her mind already felt pretty empty, but she did her best to comply with the seer's request.

"I will tell you about your future," said the gypsy, "but first you must tell me something about yourself. What is your name, child?"

"Debbie Morning," she said in the same mysterious monotone as the fortune teller.

"How old are you?"

"Eighteen. But my birthday isn't until March."

"How long have you been living in this place?"

"Eighteen years," she said with a touch of melancholy.

After a moment of silence, the gypsy abruptly said, "You are a happy person. You are a good person. You will remain a happy person for the remainder of your years. You will live in many lands. You will be married, although not to a man. You will have children, although you will not bear them. You will learn to eat lutefisk. You will die at the age of eighty-five. There is nothing more I can tell you now." The gypsy withdrew his hands from the crystal ball, which immediately went dark.

Debbie sat there stunned, tightly gripping the ball. She felt like the breath had been knocked out of her.

"You will go now," said the gypsy, breaking his eyes away from her. Now he seemed to realize that his mustache was off-kilter, and he pushed and patted it back into place.

Debbie angrily reached across the table and clawed the mustache from his face, then tore off his eyebrows, then his wig. Apart from the clothing, the man was now a blond-haired, blue-eyed, square-jawed, upright citizen, the likes of which could be found on the streets of Standard Springs any day of the week.

"You're just a big fake," said Debbie, flinging the wig to the ground. "You don't know anything about my future. You don't know anything about me at all. You make up things and tell people like it's something real. Well, it's not, you understand?"

"I understand," the man said quietly.

"You're no gypsy at all. You don't know how to work a crystal ball any better than I do. What's your name, anyway? No gypsy name, I bet."

"It's Bob Anderson."

"I knew it."

The monkey climbed up his torso, draping its arms around his neck. The man slowly stroked its head. "It's true I am not a gypsy," said the man, his voice like the man at the bank, "but that doesn't mean I can't see your soul. I tried using my given name and dressing in a suit and tie, but people wouldn't accept it. I don't think they're so much interested in the truth as finding amusement. So I changed, superficially. It would have been better, maybe more honest, not to have compromised, but the isolation was worse. Having this talent, and being alone is . . ." He shook his head, glancing away.

"Well, gosh," Debbie said. "I didn't mean to hurt your feelings. I'm normally a very nice person, if you must know."

"I do."

"I didn't understand a lot of those things you said are going to happen to me. It was like a riddle."

"Yes. But I saw no more. It will become clear as time passes, and soon it will be the past that is the puzzle."

"I'm going to be in a contest tomorrow night," said Debbie. "It's the very, very most important contest in all my life. Did you see anything about it? What did you see? Will I win?"

"I saw nothing."

"But it's all I've been thinking about since I was a little girl! I dream about it all the time: walking down the aisle, hearing the song, the crown, seated on my throne on the float. How could you not see any of that?"

He shook his head.

"What about Roger? We're going to get married and have scads of kids and live in Standard Springs forever and ever and be pretty darn happy about it! What about *that?*"

He offered no reply.

"I don't understand this at *all.*"

The man stood up, the monkey climbing onto his shoulder. His eyes didn't leave her.

"Well, thank you for your time anyway," Debbie said, rising. "I'll tell all my friends to come visit. They'll get a kick out of it."

"You are a good person and I see only light inside of you," he said as she moved for the exit. "Only light, only light . . . " he repeated as Debbie left the tent and returned to the gloom and despair of the midway.

Hanging her head, Debbie wandered through the midway, heading back toward Kiddieland. She watched the long grass flatten beneath her sneakers. All she wanted to do was find the car and go home. All she wanted at this moment was for the darkness' big steps to smother her.

"Hey, baby, wait up!"

She turned, and there were Roger and Bobby, the boyfriend clutching a fluffy pink vulture. "Look what we won," Roger said proudly, offering the bird to her. "I got it at the shootin' gallery."

He massaged his left forearm, wincing. "I took a few good hits, but I dodged 'em pretty good, didn't I, kid?"

"They shot at you a lot!" Bobby agreed.

"How did the fortune-tellin' go?" Roger asked. "Did you find out all about your future? What did he tell you, sweets?"

Debbie shrugged, hugging the vulture. "He didn't have much to say. He wasn't much of a gypsy, I guess."

"Well, I can tell you about your future right now," said Roger, placing his hand flat on his forehead and shutting his eyes. "I see a walk down a long aisle, a short ride on top of a beautiful float, the best screamin' this town has ever seen. I see riches, houses and cars and boats and gold and . . ."

"Stop it, Roger."

He lifted one eyelid and looked at her. "Don't be nervous, baby. Just be yourself and you'll do great. Heck, Molly Lovey is still lights out, you've got one of the best scars I've ever seen and you're the only contestant who had her picture on the front page of the paper. You think this is all just coincidence? So maybe you were a slow learner, but this is your time, baby. It's sittin' right there in front of you. All you have to do is reach out and take it."

Roger looped an arm around her shoulder and drew her back toward the midway. "Let's hit some of the rides for big kids, whaddaya say?"

"I don't know, Rog," said Debbie. "I'm feeling kinda tired."

"Oh, come on, don't be the poop-out Queen. When else are you going to have time to make it out here? You've got the pageant tomorrow and the parade on Saturday. How in the heck can you turn down a chance to go on the Open Bedroom Window?"

"Okay, Rog," Debbie said, mustering a smile. "You're right. I don't want to miss out." They started walking down to the dark end of the midway. "But this little guy," she said, patting Bobby's head, "is going to have to wait outside for us."

"No!" Bobby protested. "I want to go, too! I'm big enough!"

"No you aren't. Dad said. I asked him this morning. Maybe in a few years, but not tonight."

"It's not fair!"

"Don't make such a fuss," Debbie said, handing him the plush vulture. "Mom and Dad didn't allow me to go on any of the big rides until I was a teenager. I thought they were being unfair, too. Now that I'm older I can see that they were right. Gosh, if you do everything when you're seven, what is there going to be left for you to discover when you get older?"

"But I *want* to . . ."

"That's enough, you. There's nothing more to discuss so you may as well stop pouting and try to enjoy yourself."

"I'll tell you all about it when we get back," Roger promised the kid.

"Can I go on the Scary-Go-Round again?" Bobby asked in a pathetic voice.

"Our little negotiator," said Debbie. "Yes, you can go on the Scary-Go-Round again. Do you feel better now?"

He nodded mischievously, and began chewing on one of the vulture's wings.

The Open Bedroom Window was set at the terminal end of the midway, flanked by the Parking Ramp at Midnight and the Dark Backseat. Crowds milled around these attractions, and a sense of excitement and danger charged the air. OPEN BEDROOM WINDOW was spelled out in stark red letters hung over the poorly lit entrance. An oversize window with a white frame was suspended at an angle beneath the letters, nothing but darkness beyond the window.

"Now you have to promise me you'll wait right here," Debbie told Bobby at the entrance gate. "We'll be back in a few minutes. If you go wandering off there'll be no Scary-Go-Round, we'll go right home. Do you understand?"

He nodded and plopped to the ground right near the ticket taker's feet.

"Come on, Deb!" Roger said, pulling her through the gate and into the entrance of the ride.

Stepping through a black curtain, they found themselves in a short hallway that led nowhere. There were three doors with white knobs on each side of the hall. Each door had a light at its center, two of which were lit. The air smelled musty, damp. Debbie could hear a fan whirring, a muffled scream.

"You pick," said Roger.

"I don't care," she said. "Any one is okay with me."

"How about the last one on the right?"

"Fine."

They walked across the dirty floorboards to the end of the hallway. Roger reached out and gave the knob on their chosen door a twist. He nudged it open, and nodded. "All clear," he said, leading them inside.

It was a plainly furnished bedroom, lit by a lamp with a white shade on a nightstand. There was a bed with a dark blue bedspread, a dresser, and a closet on the left. Most important were the two windows, one directly opposite the bed, the other to their right. On both windows, shades were drawn, waving slightly as if in a soft night breeze.

After closing the door, Roger bounded over to the dresser and started yanking open drawers with a wild grin.

"Stay out of there," Debbie scolded him. "That doesn't belong to us."

"Sure it does. For the next few minutes, anyway." Reaching the bottom drawer, he said, "Just underwear and stuff in here. What a drag." He shut the drawers, then came back over and plopped down onto the bed, hands locked behind his head, whistling happily.

I wish I had been more stubborn with him, Debbie thought. I would much rather be home right now. I'm not in the mood for this. I don't want to be here. However, Debbie decided she did not want to spoil the experience for Roger, so she put on her best face and crawled onto the bed.

"Boy, it was a tough day at the office," Roger said. "I am really bushed. I'm going to be sawing some wood tonight, that's for sure."

Debbie pretended to yawn, and pulled up the covers to her chin, Roger following her lead. She reached out for his hand and clasped it tightly, feeling the warmth. Roger turned off the lamp. It was very dark. Debbie could hear crickets outside, but she guessed they were prerecorded.

"Good night, honey," said Roger in a deep, formal voice.

"Good night, dear," Debbie replied, yawning for real. The bed was very comfortable. She imagined they were in their very own bed in their very own house. She blinked her eyes, trying to stay alert, but felt herself slipping into sleep. She thought she should attempt to fight off the feeling, but then it was too late and she just relaxed and let the warmness overtake her. . . .

•

Debbie awoke to the sound of a knife slicing through a window screen.

As she came back to life, she realized that it was not that sound that had roused her, but Roger's voice, whispering in her ear, "Here he comes, here he comes."

Debbie opened her eyes in time to see a dark figure climbing in through the far window, the white shade passing over his dark clothing. Now he was in the room. Debbie could see the shadowy outline of a long knife in his hand. He opened a couple of the dresser drawers, throwing a handful of socks and underwear onto the floor, then turned his attention to the bed. Debbie felt Roger's body stiffen. The intruder made rough breathing noises, coming closer.

Suddenly, Debbie threw the covers off herself and jumped out of the bed. She pushed her way past the intruder, who said, "Hey, what's the deal? You've still got time left." Debbie went to the window and pulled up the shade. She looked out onto a dark field behind the midway area.

"What's wrong, peanut?" Roger called out.

Debbie climbed out the window, which in fact had no screen at all, and began walking swiftly through the deep grasses, the dew soaking her sneakers, not looking back, tears streaming down her face.

Then, in the middle of the field, she pulled up and knelt down, hands clenched, head lowered.

She heard a sweeping sound in the grasses behind her, and then felt Roger's arm around her, his face close by. "What's the matter, sweets? Why are you crying? Were you scared?"

Debbie looked at him plaintively and said, "No."

15

Debbie woke just after dawn on Friday morning, flies swarming in her stomach. She had slept fitfully, not dreaming, nervousness welling up inside of her. The most important of all days had finally arrived. She felt nauseated, on the verge of throwing up, when she climbed out of bed and went to the bathroom. Looking at her face in the mirror, she frowned with dismay. The wonderful scar on her forehead, certain to be the hit of the show, was already fading. Its scarlet hues were muted, and a lumpy scab had formed where there once was a swell gouge. Boy, that's really something, she thought in frustration. Not only am I not scared, I'm a quick healer to boot.

After getting dressed, Debbie went downstairs and saw that she was the first one up. She eschewed her usual glass of liquid eye opener and headed straight outside. It was cool, and a little early morning fog still hung in the trees and above the glistening lawns. She began walking, her mind working on what she needed to do to be victorious tonight.

There were some aspects of the pageant she could prepare for and some she could not. In the question-and-answer session with the judges, for instance, the responses were unrehearsed, and the best strategy was to keep on her toes and be confident when speaking even if the words that tumbled out of her mouth were gibberish. The screaming competition, on the other hand, was something she could and did prepare for. Her throat had improved a good deal since her last visit with Mrs. Toddler; all traces of hoarseness had disappeared. Now the routine was to drink a glass of hot lemon and honey water approximately two hours prior to the start of the pageant, then warm up her vocal chords with a shriek or two before it was her turn. For lack of a better alternative, she had chosen to visualize her fictitious bad dream about the stinging bugs on the apple, more for Mrs. Toddler's sake than with any thought that it might actually be effective.

Debbie rounded the corner, going down the quiet sidewalks on Pain Lane, skipping over the angleworms that lay writhing on the pavement.

Fear, fear, fear, she reminded herself. Talent was certainly important, but when it came down to choosing a Scream Queen, Debbie speculated that the judges were looking for someone who best fit the image, who carried the spirit of Serial Killer Days within her. I can do that, she tried to convince herself. Just for a couple of hours, I can do that.

She came to the downtown area, at the corner of Main and Pain, and took a left, going past the newspaper office, Hamp's Hardware, the jailhouse.

The one area she felt some trepidation about was the talent competition, simply because the poem she would be reciting was new and she feared that she would forget the words. It wasn't that hard of a poem, and it sure was memorable, so repetition to the point of numbness was the key.

"Once, if I recollect right," Debbie recited aloud. No, that's wrong, she thought. There should be more of a pause after "once." Just relax, take your time.

She rounded the corner.

"Once, if I recollect right," she said again, "my life was a Sunday dinner with all the fixins, where every heart said howdy, where . . ."

"Every brewski flowed!"

Debbie stopped, stunned. She looked in all directions, saw nothing, and wondered if she was still asleep. "One night I gave Beauty a big ol' hug . . ." she continued.

"And she didn't feel too swell!" a male voice boomed out from a high window on the building at her right. The jail, she realized.

"Who said that?" Debbie called out.

"I did."

"Jim Bowie, is that you?"

"Who's Jim Bowie?"

"But you know Ole Rimbaud . . ."

"I don't know Ole Rimbaud, my dear, I *am* Ole Rimbaud."

●

Debbie couldn't believe it. Ole Rimbaud was *here,* right in her own hometown! But what had he done to land himself behind bars? She knew it must be a mistake; her idol would never lie or cheat or steal.

"Is it really you?" Debbie asked, still not quite willing to accept her good fortune. "Are you really Ole?"

"Straight from Paristown to you," he said. "You've read my work, I take it."

"Oh, I'm a big fan," she gushed. "Your biggest fan anywhere, well maybe not everywhere, but most definitely your biggest fan in Standard Springs."

"How do you like the new book?"

"Oh, it's wonderful. I . . ."

"This is darn foolish," he interrupted. "I can't even see you, and I'm standing on my tiptoes on my cot. Where can we meet?"

"Uh, I guess I should come see you. I mean, I don't see how . . ."

"I'm not in the fix I appear to be," he said jovially. "I'll explain later. Just tell me someplace we can meet, away from crowds, if you can manage it, and what time and I'll be there."

"I suppose we could meet in a park."

"Sounds dandy. What park?"

"Victory Park, I guess. It's just a couple of blocks from here. I told my teacher I would stop by her place at nine, so we could meet at ten, if that suits your schedule. I'll wait by the flagpole so you'll know it's me."

"Sounds peachy. By the way, what's your name?"

"I'm Debbie. Debbie Morning."

"See you soon, Debbie Morning."

"Bye, good-bye, Mr. Rimbaud, sir."

"Say, Debbie Morning? You still there?"

"Yes, I'm here."

"I'm trying to keep a low profile while I'm in town, don't want to get mobbed, you know, so I sure would appreciate it if you'd keep all this to yourself."

"I won't tell anyone."

"Appreciate it, darlin'."

Debbie wandered away from the jailhouse in a daze. She tried to resume her recital, but the words were all jumbled in her head. Her heart was flipping something wild. She was nervous and happy and almost frightened. What am I going to say to him? she thought. Did I act too much like a starstruck fan? I want him to take me seriously. I'm not just some lovesick poetry reader; I really understand him, at least I think I do. What if he turns out to be a big jerk? What if he thinks *I'm* a big jerk? Gosh, I don't know what I'd do. Maybe I shouldn't chance it; maybe I shouldn't meet him at all, ever.

Attempting to reign in her thoughts, Debbie saw that the clock on the bank still only said seven-thirty. As she headed up Vine Street, she decided she would not go home but instead sit by the pond for a while before visiting Mrs. Toddler. Debbie did not want to face any questions this morning or be asked to run an errand. I don't want another day of lies, she thought. Better to avoid the whole darn thing.

When she reached the pond across the way from Mrs. Toddler's house, Debbie found her usual flat, worn, contemplating-the-world boulder. A pair of ducks dove under the water at the other end of the pond. Water bugs skittered across the surface. A turtle sunning itself on a log down the shore eyed her carefully. Debbie sat hugging her knees, her eyes shut, and began to feel more like herself again. This must be the best place in the whole world, she thought. I should have told Ole to meet me here. I could take him here later. But a part of her was glad that she had kept the spot to herself, even as much as she adored the Paristown bard.

I do hope we become friends, she thought dreamily, tapping the warm water with the tips of her fingers. We could go places together, places I've never been before, and he could read his new poems to me. Maybe he'd even write a poem about me. Maybe we'd even . . . Golly, get hold of yourself, girl, Debbie thought, opening her eyes. You just met the fellow five seconds ago and already you're going to be with him forever. I can't help it, she told her sensible self, I'm in love.

"Is that you, Debbie?"

Debbie turned. It was Mrs. Toddler, walking down the path from her house. Debbie waved.

"I thought I saw you go by," her teacher said, coming up to her. "You should have invited yourself in. You didn't have to wait until nine."

"I wanted to sit and think for a while," said Debbie. "I like it here so much. I'd live here if I could. I'd build myself a little shack on a raft in the middle of the pond and let the froggies sing me to sleep every night. That's a *very* nice dress, Mrs. Toddler." It was white chenille with black pearls.

"Thank you, dear."

"I'm not really nervous about tonight," said Debbie. "I was before, but now I'm okay. I'm just going to go out there and do my best and whatever happens, happens, right?"

Touching her student's forehead, the craggy scar, Mrs. Toddler said, "How on earth did you get this?"

"I fell down. I thought it was going to get infected, but it doesn't look like it will now." Debbie made a face. "I'm a quick healer."

Mrs. Toddler fussed over the wound a few seconds longer, then said, "How's your throat feeling?"

"Really good. Not hoarse at all. I'm going to make my usual honey and lemon concoction before I leave tonight, just to make sure."

Brushing off a spot on the rock, Mrs. Toddler sat down. She looked out at the pond. "So how did your visit with Gussie go?"

"Well, she's a very sweet person," said Debbie. "She made me feel right at home, just like part of the family. And what a lovely old house. No complaints here!"

"She wasn't able to help you, dear, was she?" Mrs. Toddler asked quietly.

Debbie solemnly shook her head. "No, ma'am."

"Perhaps it's just as well. You need to find your own fear within yourself. Nobody can do it for you." The mentor gazed narrowly at Debbie. "I take it you haven't changed your mind about the talent portion of the contest."

"The poem's going really well," Debbie said hopefully. "I think I've got it all memorized now." She desperately wanted to tell Mrs. Toddler that Ole Rimbaud was in town this very minute and that she was going to be seeing him in a little over an hour, but Debbie beat down the urge, remembering her promise to her hero.

"Are you going to use any blood or other props?"

"It's really not that type of poem, Mrs. Toddler," said Debbie. "I don't want anything to distract from his words. It's such a wonderful poem that I think it will stand just fine on its own."

"Well, you certainly still have as good a chance to win as any of the other girls. From what I understand Molly Lovey hasn't stirred since she was struck down."

"I visited her a couple of days ago," Debbie said. "I didn't think she looked very perky."

"You visited her?" Mrs. Toddler said, smiling. "That was very sporting of you, Debra. We should make sure the judges know. An act of benevolence like that could clinch Miss Congeniality for you."

"I just wish she would get better. The contest won't be the same without her."

The two chatted for a while longer, as the sun splashed across the surface of the pond, then around nine-thirty Debbie departed, getting a good luck hug from her teacher. She wanted to leave herself plenty of time to get to the park; it simply would not do to keep someone as great and famous as Ole Rimbaud waiting.

Debbie strode quickly back down Vine Street. When she reached the main drag, she could see that the town was already humming with activity: strangers strolling along looking for bargains at the sidewalk sales, sitting on benches with maps and sodas and their sullen children punching black balloons. It was hard not to feel happy, and proud. For on these special days the eyes of the whole tri-county area was on Standard Springs. Even some folks from Katoville and St. CanDo were probably here.

See, it's not such a small town after all, Debbie imagined herself bragging to the visitors. There's so much to see and do: You can visit the historic sites, attend the theater, go to the parade.

And you must catch the sack race.

Just don't ask what's in the sack.

16

Standing beneath the flag pole in Victory Park, Debbie saw a man enter the park, walking down the bike path, scuffing his shoes in the dirt. He was dressed in a long blue shirt and jeans, sunglasses, and a black baseball cap pulled low. He didn't seem to be headed in any particular direction at first, but his circuitous route was bringing him closer and closer and suddenly Debbie realized that the man was not merely aimlessly wandering through the park, but had a very definite destination and was in fact . . .

"Hello." The dark-haired man stopped right at Debbie's side. He was standing at an angle, not looking directly at her, as if he was waiting for the light at Main and Pain to change and had greeted her just to be neighborly.

"Hi," said Debbie, glancing at him. She felt goose bumps on her arms. Was it really him? She couldn't believe her eyes. He was taller than she had pictured him in her mind.

"Boy, it feels good to get outdoors," he said. "I've been cooped up in there all week. Can't complain too much, though; the food's plenty good."

"What did you do?" she whispered.

"Aw, don't be scared of me," he said. "I was an apple thief, now I'm king of this here hill. They don't even know who I really am; I gave them a fake name."

"They put you in jail for stealing apples?"

"It was just one apple and I only ate a couple bites from it.

How was I supposed to know they were prize winners? That old woman almost killed me, she had a shotgun on me until the cops showed up. I love her, though, and I know I'll write a poem about her someday."

"You must be talking about Mrs. Flatwire. Gosh, you sure picked the wrong apple orchard to raid. I'm surprised she didn't have any 'No Trespassing' signs out."

"Well, she may well have," said the poet.

"I'm such a big fan of yours," Debbie said, trying not to fawn over him. "I must have read every book you ever wrote."

"Do you have *Unluckytown?*"

"Gosh, no. I've never even heard of it. When did it come out?"

"A couple of years ago. It was a very limited edition, printed on corn husks. I'll send you a copy."

"That would be wonderful." Debbie tried to keep herself under control. Am I talking too much? she wondered. Am I sounding too immature? He sure is nice. Just as nice as I imagined.

"You know, Mr. Rimbaud," said Debbie, "I'm going to be reading one of your poems tonight at the Pageant of Fear."

"I'm right flattered. What will you be reading?"

" 'Once, If I Recollect Right.' It's one of my favorites. I hope you'll be able to come to the pageant." Don't be so aggressive, Debbie scolded herself. "Oh, I'm sorry. I bet you must have other plans, a famous person like you, readings and autograph parties and receptions?"

"I'd like to make it to the pageant," he said, "but I have to keep my, uh, public appearances pretty limited."

"I never thought you'd come to my hometown, never dreamed I'd be able to meet you. What brought you to town, anyway? I thought you had a hog farm in Paristown."

"Doin' research on my next book. Writing my impressions as I travel along, from one end of Atlantis County to the other. My neighbor is taking care of my hogs while I'm gone. I'd never neglect them. If I had to choose between them and my poems, I don't know which I'd pick, and that's the natural truth."

Debbie sat down in the grass; all the excitement seemed to

have drained the strength from her legs. To her utter surprise, Ole Rimbaud seated himself as well, his knees not more than three inches from her own. Debbie tried to think of something to say to him, and finally she blurted out, to her immediate embarrassment, "So how long are you going to be behind bars?"

"Just until the end of the week. You might say I was offered a very generous plea bargain."

"Oh, that's nice." She looked away.

"Your sheriff has been right neighborly to me."

Debbie looked at him again. "I told people about you," she said.

"Told people?"

"I went to the Cities the other night. Please don't tell my mom or she'll have heart failure."

"Hog farmer's honor," Ole said, raising his hand.

"I found this bar where you could get on stage and recite poetry. I read one of yours. I had orange juice, too, with a straw and everything. There were some people there, they called themselves poets. Jim Bowie and Latisha and Lazy Larry and I went back to their apartment and we talked and stuff and we had a lot of fun. I told them all about you, everything I know at any rate. They sounded really interested in meeting you. They put out a magazine, called *Grow Up* or something. They want you to contribute."

"Well, that sure makes my heart glad."

"I'd never been to the Cities before, except once when I saw a mummy. Have you ever been there?"

"A couple of times, but it's been years. I'm not much on cities. I got turned around every time I turned around."

"Me, too!" Debbie said. This is so great, she thought. We have so much in common and we've only been talking for a few minutes. Maybe I should invite him to the pond. He could meet Mrs. Toddler and then maybe she'd understand why I want to recite his poem in the pageant.

"You know, Mr. Rimbaud," she began shyly, "I was wondering if you . . ."

138

"WOOOHOOOO!!!"

The yell which suddenly broke the morning quietude came from the opposite side of the park, but it almost seemed to shake the ground where they sat. A grackle in the grass took flight. A gopher skittered into its hole. The sun broke through the clouds and the few people in the park began to gravitate toward the old man, who was still whooping and hopping up and down and dancing in circles and generally carrying on unlike many individuals from that era Debbie had encountered.

"I wonder what the deal is over there?" Ole said. "Come on, let's take a look."

Disappointed yet relieved that she had avoided the chance of a possible rejection, Debbie tagged along. The crowd had grown rapidly in the moments following the man's celebration, word spreading through town via some subconscious channel, each soul linked together with tin cans and string.

People were gathering around Junior Sasser, who wore a smile like a baby. He was standing in the baseball field at home plate, the dish overturned, a small hole in the reddish dirt revealed. He was holding something aloft in one hand, but Debbie couldn't make it out. In his other hand he gripped a forked stick. She noticed that Griff Grimes had joined the throng, shouldering his way to the inner circle.

"I sure showed that brother of mine!" Junior shouted gleefully. "I sure showed him!"

"Mr. Sasser, a couple of questions, please," said Griff Grimes, flipping open a notepad. "What were you thinking when you found the prize?"

"Wasn't thinkin' at all. It's not a thinkin' job, you see."

"How did you know where to look?"

"My friend right here told me," said Junior, waving his stick. "It told me the prize was in the park somewhere. Just took me a little longer to hone in on it than I figured."

"You used a dowsing rod?" Griff inquired. "I thought you could only find water with one of those."

"Oh no, not at all. Water is just *one* of many things you can find. Your standard dowsin' rod can be used to find pretty near everything, if you put your mind to it. Did you know Ponce D. Lion discovered the Fountain of Youth with one of these beauties?" He nodded. "It's true."

"What is it exactly?" asked Griff, peering at the prize, which Junior now had cupped in his hand. "A thumb?"

"Naw, looks like a pinky to me. What do you folks think?" Junior displayed the severed digit for all to see, and the spectators for the most part affirmed his speculation. Then a mild argument broke out over whether it was a lefty or a righty, which was silly, Debbie thought. Anybody with half an eye could see that it was a lefty, for goodness sake.

Just then a humming noise could be heard, followed by a whoosh of air that Debbie felt sweep across her legs. A dull green saucer floated to the edges of the crowd. A red-haired man in Bermuda shorts, Junior's older brother, Leon, exited from the rear hatch, hands in his pockets, accompanied by his frisky bulldog, jowls knocking off the white dandelion tops as he chugged along. The crowd parted, allowing Leon to pass, and then it closed around the brothers, who now stood face to face.

The Sassers eyed each other for a moment before a big grin broke over Leon's face and he extended his right hand, which Junior tentatively clasped. "You have my heartiest congratulations, little brother," said Leon. "You sure outsmarted me this year! That ol' saucer was no match for you. I guess it's back to the drawing board for me."

"Uh, well, thanks kindly, big brother," replied Junior, looking uncertain. "That's right nice of you to be a good sport about it."

"Technology sure fouled things up this time," Leon said, laughing. "Never thought they'd hide the prize under home plate."

"But your Soil Sonar . . ."

"Can't see through a rubberized surface," Leon explained. "Blocked it good. I never had a chance." Now addressing the crowd, he said, "Let it be known that my little brother won fair and square. Let's give three cheers for Junior! Come on, everybody! Hip hip!"

"HOORAY!"

On the third hooray Debbie noticed that her father had appeared on the scene. As Leon headed back to his saucer, Mr. Morning went over to him and the two men began talking.

"I think I'll get a poem out of this," Ole said, as the crowd broke up and he and Debbie strolled through the park. "In fact, I'll write it right now. Would you like that, Debbie?"

"Wow, I've never seen anyone write a poem before," she said. "At least not a famous poet."

"Do you write poems yourself?" he asked.

"No," she said quickly. "I'm more of the cheerleader type, I'm afraid. I like to read 'em, though."

"This one I'll call 'The Pinky of Youth,' " he said, stopping, and then began reciting in a resonant voice: "Oh the pinky of youth / clipped off in its prime! / those dark, jagged passages / the desperation of youth / the passage of time / oh the rotted passage of time." He started walking again. "That's the end of that one."

"You just made that up?" Debbie asked in amazement.

"Sure did. Let me remind you that I am a professional."

"Oh, I didn't doubt you could do it."

They walked together in silence for a time, and then Ole said, "I'd better get back. My keepers are probably gettin' nervous."

"Oh," Debbie said, feeling her heart sink. She saw a drained pond, a dowsing rod breaking, a lost and lonely heart, and a pinky, just lost.

"But we'll be seeing one another again," he said, smiling cryptically, and then left her side, heading back to the jailhouse.

Debbie stood and watched him recede, not moving until he pulled open the door to the lock up and disappeared inside.

"The passage of time, oh the rotted passage of time," she said softly, hugging herself, and then she sighed and started for home.

17

You'll never believe what happened!" Mrs. Morning announced as Debbie came in the door.

"What happened, Mom?" said Debbie, plopping onto the couch.

"Well, Junior Sasser found the prize . . ."

"I know, Mom. I was just there. He sure was . . ."

". . . only it wasn't the prize he found at all."

"It *wasn't* the prize?" Debbie said in disbelief. "He sure acted like he found it."

"Well, just between you and me—I told Mrs. Gear that it would go no further, so don't tell anyone—I understand that it was actually Junior's brother who found the prize several days ago at the fairgrounds."

"What was it Junior found then?"

Her mom ran her right index finger along the base of her left pinky, making a cutting noise.

"Leon . . ."

Mrs. Morning nodded knowingly.

"So what happened to the original prize?"

"Well, Mrs. Gear wasn't sure about that, but Leon's dog, Boss, is suspect number one from what I understand."

"Wow," said Debbie.

"It's quite an act of brotherly love and something we should all take a lesson from."

"I'm just amazed at how fast news travels sometimes," said Debbie.

Her mother sat on the edge of the couch. "You were up and out early this morning."

"A case of the jitters, I guess. I walked all over. I stopped in to see Mrs. Toddler. She said to say hi."

"She's so nice," said her mother. "She's been to the Middle East, you know. I think she once dated a Shiite."

Debbie found herself unable to sit still as judgment hour neared. She checked her dress every few minutes to make sure it was perfect: no stray threads, no unseen tears, no spots or stains. She shut her eyes and recited her poem. She limbered up. She made another futile attempt to paste a frightened look on her affable mug.

"Debbie Sue Morning," her mother said on one of Debbie's trips through the kitchen, "if you don't settle down you're going to be in no shape to do much of anything tonight. Why don't you watch television or go in the backyard and play with your brother?" She used a spatula to turn over a pan of cocktail weenies on the stove.

"Sorry, Mom. I guess I'm getting pretty worked up. I'll go outside for a while. Could you let me know when it's three? I want to whip up my special treatment for my throat then."

"I'll give you a holler."

"Thanks." Debbie skipped out the back door. She found Bobby in the sandbox at the corner of the yard, a shade tree overhanging the area. He was on his hands and knees, using a yellow beach shovel to dig a hole in the sand.

"Whatcha looking for, kid?" Debbie asked, leaning over him, hands on her knees.

He mumbled something and kept up his vigorous excavation.

"Don't go too deep or you'll strike snake oil," Debbie joked.

Bobby stopped digging and looked up at her. "Really?"

"No, of course not." Her brow furrowed. "At least I don't think so."

Shoveling out one more scoopful of earth, Bobby stuck his

hand in the hole and proclaimed gleefully, "Found it!" He held up what appeared to be a sand-coated cocktail weenie. He scampered back to the house, waving the prize above his head, proudly announcing his discovery at the top of his tiny lungs. She heard her mom tell Bobby to lower his voice and that she wouldn't give him any more weenies if all he was going to do was play with them. This threat seemed to work, and a subdued little brother came back outside and sat on the step, inspecting an anthill.

Debbie lounged under the tree for a time, returning to the house when her mother called her. She put water on to boil, then took a lemon from the refrigerator and opened the cupboard to get a jar of honey. Her hand hesitated as she reached for the jar, feeling a moment of dread at the memory of the suicidal grackles. But this honey jar featured a grinning baby bear slopping a mitt full of the tasty goop into his mouth, reassuring her.

"Need some help?" her mother asked.

"No, Mom, I'm fine." When the water reached a near boil, she poured it into a mug, then split the lemon in half and squeezed it in her fist, letting the juice drip into the glass. She scooped in two spoonfuls of honey and waited for it to dissolve, stirring slightly. She took a sip, added a little more honey. Another sip. Perfect, she thought, and went upstairs.

Debbie ran a hot bath and set the mug on the edge of the tub. After placing a white towel near the steaming tub, she undressed and climbed in. Immersing herself up to her neck, she brought the towel into the tub, soaking it and wrapping it around her throat. Boy, that's good, she thought, taking a drink of hot honey and lemon, feeling the liquid course down her gullet.

When the water turned lukewarm and the mug was drained, Debbie climbed out of the tub, quickly toweled off, and dressed, so as not to catch a chill. She saw that it was getting close to four o'clock, and Miss Exeter had insisted that the contestants arrive at the high school no later than four-fifteen. Debbie laid her gown and leotard out on the bed, slipping them into a dry cleaning bag, and gave her shoes a final buff.

Examining herself in the bathroom mirror, wiping a circle on the glass to clear the steam, Debbie wished she could do something about the wound on her forehead. Overnight it had worsened dramatically; the swelling was gone, even the scab now had taken on a benign hue.

I could change that, she thought. Debbie took a nail file and pressed it to the wound, trying to figure out which angle of cut would produce the most effect with the least amount of pain. Would a jabbing or scraping motion work best? she wondered. I could call Miss Exeter and see what she thought. But then her nerve suddenly waned and she dropped the file into the sink.

The phone rang.

"Debbie Sue!" her mother called from downstairs. "It's Roger!"

Debbie picked up the phone by her bed. "Rog, is that you?"

"How's my queen doin' today?"

"I'm just about ready to go. You're going to be there, aren't you?"

"Wouldn't miss it, sweets."

"Hey, I was in the park this morning and something funny happened with the Sasser brothers," she said. "It seems that . . ."

"I know all about it," he broke in.

"It seems like everybody knows about it. Wasn't it something?"

"Yes, it was," he said solemnly.

●

Mr. Morning was scheduled to arrive home by four to take Debbie to school. She had convinced him that it wouldn't do for a Scream Queen contestant to ride to the pageant in a clown car.

"Dad's here!" Debbie said, peeking out the front window as the maroon sedan pulled into the driveway right as the clock on the living room wall chimed four. She gathered up her clothes. Her mother gave her a hug. "Good luck, dear. We'll be rooting for you."

"Thanks, Mom. I'll do my best."

Debbie hurried out to the car, grinning at her dad, who waved and gave her a tense smile in return. She opened the back door and carefully placed her clothes and shoes on the seat, then hopped in the front.

"The big night's finally here," he said. "I'm very proud of you."

"Thanks for driving me, Dad," she said. "Are you going to be able to make it tonight?"

"Count on it," he said. "I've got a meeting at six, last minute kind of deal, but hopefully it won't last long. I may miss the opening, though."

"Oh, that's okay. It's just a dumb dance number. The real exciting stuff doesn't come 'til later."

When they reached the school, Debbie gave her dad a hug and retrieved her clothes from the backseat. He pulled away, and as she was turning to head up the sidewalk to the main entrance, another car drove up to the curb. Someone opened the passenger door and got out, carrying a garment bag and shoes.

Debbie wasn't sure if she should hurry into the building, pretending that she had not seen her competitor, or if she should stop and exhibit some good old-fashioned Scream Queen camaraderie. Her initial impulse was to avoid the girl, because, heck, Debbie thought, she was mean to me first. Why should I be nice to her? Why should I treat her any differently than she did me?

"Hi, Samantha," Debbie said, as the car pulled away. "You sure are looking fine tonight."

Samantha eyed her warily. "Thanks. Nice contusion. Did you just get that?"

"Well, it is pretty new. You should have seen it a couple of days ago, though. I can't believe how quickly it healed."

"That happens to me, too," Samantha said with a trace of empathy. "Once I had a bruise on my eye, it was big and swollen and everything, but then the next morning you could hardly tell that anything had happened. Boy, was I mad!"

"What did you do?"

"What *could* I do?"

They walked together up the sidewalk to the entrance. The school halls were quiet and dim and the girls headed down the corridor, past the trophy case, to the large dressing room behind the stage. The other contestants were already getting dressed, combing their hair and chatting. They looked over as Debbie and Samantha entered the room.

There was a long silence.

"Hi, guys," Lois finally said.

"Hi, everyone," Debbie said tentatively.

"Wow, Debbie," Tabby Sorensen said. "Where'd you get the gash?"

The girls came over to Debbie and oohed and aahed at her fading wound.

"Oh, it's not all that great," Debbie said. "You should have seen it yesterday."

"Don't be so modest," Samantha said with a smile.

"Well, look at you, Tabby," said Debbie. "You've got a pretty swell laceration there yourself." The other girl sported a deep red slash tracking from her shoulder to her upper chest area.

"Thanks. Do you think it will be noticeable from the audience?"

"Maybe not from the back row," Debbie said, "but you can bet the judges will sit up and take notice."

"I was going to get a scar," said Lois, "but I was too busy."

"Oh, you're just a big chicken," Tabby teased her.

"Maybe it's still not too late," Lois mused.

"Anybody seen Miss Exeter?" Debbie asked.

"Miss Exeter has arrived," said a familiar husky voice at the door.

They all turned their attention to the door where Penelope Exeter was standing, dressed in her formal prison guard uniform. She came into the room, giving them a quick inspection. "I'm seeing some fine scarring here today. I'm glad you girls showed the initiative. It'll serve you well later in life." She gently touched Debbie's forehead. *Very* nice, Morning."

"Thank you, ma'am."

"When you girls finish dressing," Miss Exeter announced, "meet me on stage and we can go over some last-minute details. Please don't dawdle. It may seem early, but before you know it your parents and friends will be taking their seats on the other side of this wall and you'll be out there kicking up a storm. Any questions?"

"When is Kirk Potz going to be coming?" Lois asked.

"Mr. Potz should be arriving shortly."

After Miss Exeter departed, Debbie hung up her gown, shed her clothes, and tugged on her black leotard, the mutual style choice for the opening number. It seemed to be a little tight and she was glad she had not sampled the cocktail weenies. As Debbie brushed her hair in front of one of the small mirrors that were propped up on the tables, she was disturbed to see that her hair was hiding the edge of her scar. Hmm, she thought, that's not the best. She hunted around and found a container of gel, and applied a dollop to her hair in the trouble area. There, that should do it.

Maybe the scar will be okay after all, she thought. Look at all the compliments I've gotten already. Compared to the other girls, my wound stands up pretty darn well. Maybe I'm just being too hard on myself. I never thought of myself as a perfectionist. I always thought I was just a regular person. A perfectionist. Does that fit me? I always get mad when my clapping slips out of rhythm with the other cheerleaders. I always prefer to have my peas lined up in rows on my plate. Wow, a *perfectionist*. I'll have to tell Dad.

Debbie did some stretching exercises, making an *O* over her head with her arms, bringing her knees up to her chest, extending her face muscles into a big frown.

She glanced at the other contestants, who were involved in the same type of exertions, trying to pick up some cue that would help her once the contest began. It was difficult to gauge their expressions. Was that the natural tension common before an important competition or were they putting their worst faces on, imagining who knows what in their minds? Debbie felt some mild nervousness about performing in front of an audience, but it remained an undercurrent because she was so preoccupied with concentrating on her dance moves and recital.

When everyone had finished dressing, the contestants trooped out through the stage door, went through the wings, and filed out onto the stage. There were a pair of workers just below the front of the stage, stringing a line of electrical cable. A handful of people were setting up folding chairs at the back of the gymnasium, the clatter of metal echoing throughout the empty space. A small boy was sliding across the polished floor on his knees. It almost seems like a normal practice session, Debbie thought.

"Okay, girls, listen up!" said Miss Exeter, who was pacing back and forth at the foot of the stage. "Now we all realize what's at stake here tonight. One and only one of you four young women will be wearing the crown when you leave this auditorium. But in my eyes you are all part of the same family. You are upholding a very special tradition, no matter how well you do here tonight. It's like I tell the cons: Some of you may be muggers, some of you may be drunk drivers, some of you may be wife beaters, but you are all part of the big PowPow family. You are . . ."

There was a stir among the contestants.

Debbie didn't catch on at first, but Miss Exeter apparently realized that she no longer gripped the girls' attention. She frowned and turned to look out at the expanse of the gymnasium.

Debbie still couldn't see what the commotion was about. She whispered to Samantha, "What's going on?"

"I don't believe it," Samantha said in a quietly disturbed tone. *"I don't believe it."*

Then Debbie saw what the commotion was all about.

"I don't believe it," said Debbie.

Molly Lovey was in the building.

·

STIGMATA
FOR A
HIGH SCHOOL
GIRL

·

18

Arvid Morning arrived at the courthouse late, just after six, and he was not in a bureaucratic mood at all. Back in his downtown office a maze of multicolored index cards papered one wall; even though it was only a day until the parade, there were still late entries to place, refinements to be made. As expected, the Nodal High marching band had finally, grudgingly accepted the committee's offer. So the bands were set. But this morning, for instance, a group of local wags informed Arvid that they had a "float" they wanted to enter consisting of a manure spreader manned by individuals wearing paper masks representing various political candidates. In most cases, Arvid would simply turn down such a tardy entry, but he was amused by this one enough to make an exception.

His other source of irritation was the timing of this meeting, which had the potential of overlapping the beginning of the pageant. He had promised Debbie he would make it, and he was unwilling to back off his word. All the Mayor said on the phone was to get down to the courthouse right away. Whatever the purpose of this gathering, it darn well better be important, he thought.

Arvid entered the courthouse, striding briskly through the main corridor and down the stairs to their semisecret meeting room. As he came into the room, he noticed that the assemblage, Judge Flail, Sheriff Eeha, Lucas the city manager, and Mayor Sellit appeared to be waiting for him.

"Hello, boys," said Arvid, shutting the door and taking a seat at the table. "I hope this won't take long," he said. "You fellows know the pageant is going to start in less than an hour, don't you?"

"Couldn't be helped," said the Mayor. He looked tense, agitated. "Arv, we've got a real situation on our hands."

"Situation?"

"A decision," the Judge added.

"What happened?" Arvid asked with a wan, puzzled look.

The Mayor gazed at Sheriff Eeha. "Do you want to tell him, Ned?"

Clearing his throat, the Sheriff said, "Yes, I'll tell him. This meeting is my doing, after all." The Sheriff clasped his hands on the table, studying Arvid with a deadpan stare, and said, "Well, it involves our designated serial killer, the fella we brought in for stealing Mrs. Flatwire's apples."

"Don't tell me he escaped," Mr. Morning pleaded. "Please don't tell me he escaped. The parade is tomorrow. There's no . . ."

"No, no, no, it ain't like that," said Sheriff Eeha. "He's snug in jail, been there all week. Seems not to mind, actually."

Arvid shut his eyes, the words soothing his panic.

"The problem is," the Sheriff said, "is that I have a suspicion that our honored guest really is our very own serial killer."

Arvid stared at him narrowly but said nothing.

"I think he's been coming to Standard Springs every summer for the past twenty-one years and making a killing," the Sheriff continued. "Only this year we caught him as he came into town. It was a fluke. Or maybe he got tired of the whole mess and wanted to be caught."

Arvid glanced at the other town officials, who appeared as helpless as he felt inside. He returned his attention to the Sheriff. "I'm assuming you've got some proof on this."

"Nothing that ties him directly to any of the killings, but enough to hold him through Saturday night. That way, if he is the killer, there won't be a victim by Sunday morning. It's just a matter of holding onto him a few more hours than we planned."

"Okay, but why do you think he's the serial killer?"

"Number one, he's a stranger in town, who showed up the week of Serial Killer Days. My deputy reported that Mrs. Flatwire said the fella told her he was in town *for* Serial Killer Days. Number two, he had a notebook on him, filled with bizarro writing."

"Bizarro writing?"

"Psycho stuff. Heck, how'd that one go?" Sheriff Eeha peered at the ceiling for guidance. "Oh, the stabbing something or other, hearts and fires and this or that, the rotted, oh heck I can't remember now. But it was a pretty sick business. Obviously the product of a dangerous mind."

"Is that all?"

"Then there's my deputy. He used sort of an off trail investigative technique, but it seemed to work just fine. Told him the stranger was the serial killer, no ifs, ands or . . ."

"What did he use?"

"A dowsing rod."

"Oh, great," said Arvid.

"He said he pointed the dowsing stick right at the prisoner and it went nuts."

"That's a pretty iffy deal, don't you think, Ned?"

"Well, it worked for Junior Sasser," the Sheriff said defensively. "He found the prize with it, just this morning."

"No, he didn't," said Arvid. "Leon found it a few days ago. He was just trying to be kind to his little brother."

"Well, I hadn't heard that."

"Are you sure this doesn't have anything to do with your re-election, Sheriff Eeha?" Arvid asked. "I know Rodney Owl is spreading the word around that you're not doing your job."

"I already asked him that," said the Mayor. "Now you heard it and we heard it and it seems like we have a decision to make."

"But a decision that shouldn't be made without possessing full and complete information on the matter," interjected the city manager.

"Full and complete information?" asked Arvid.

"What do you mean?" the Mayor said.

"Let me explain," replied Lucas, gathering up sheets of paper and uncapping a wide felt tip pen. He quickly sketched a pair of graphs. "Now it's my opinion that what we're facing here is a purely technical decision. It's not something we should get all emotional over." Upon completing his drawings he recapped his pen. "There are clearly two avenues to pursue here, represented by the following charts."

Lucas held up the first chart, which showed a line beginning at the top left-hand corner of the page and angling steeply to the bottom right corner. "Chart A here is a depiction of what would happen to the local economy if the killer was captured resulting in the end of Serial Killer Days."

"You're making a mighty big assumption there," the Sheriff pointed out, "that if there was no serial killer there would be no Serial Killer Days."

"Well, I guess I am making that assumption," Lucas said. "I guess I assumed it was clear that interest in the celebration would wane if the whole center of the celebration was eliminated."

"Lucas is right," said the Mayor. "It would be like Christmas without Santy Claus. Can you picture such a thing? I sure can't."

"If you'll grant me that assumption," Lucas continued, "then this is the calamitous effect the termination of Serial Killer Days would have on Main Street. There would be no reason for anyone to come to Standard Springs anymore. Our businesses count on Serial Killer Days to bring in the customers. We've talked before about the factors already hurting our economy: the farm situation, the Big Big Store, the exodus of our youth."

"It is a *terrible* situation," said the Mayor.

"Now, here on Chart B is Standard Springs if the serial killer is not caught and Serial Killer Days remains part of the fabric of our town for many years to come." Lucas held up the second chart, which showed a Pikes Peak magnitude incline.

The Mayor whistled.

"What I didn't include in my calculations," said Lucas, "is the enhancement of the Serial Killer Days celebration in the fiscal years to come. I'm talking about our proposed change of the town name to Serial Killer, the possibility of corporate sponsorship, direct mail catalogs, whatever notions we can imagine."

"But we can't let him go!" Sheriff Eeha protested. "I caught him fair and square!"

"Sheriff, I wonder if you're more interested in your own ambitions than in the welfare of this town," said the Mayor scoldingly.

"But it's an ethical question, ain't it?" said the Sheriff. "I'm not sure you have a chart for it, but when all this gets boiled down, what we're proposing is never apprehending the serial killer, and if we do catch him, letting him go so he can kill again."

There was a long silence in the room, then the Mayor said, "Well, wouldn't there be more suffering in Standard Springs if there was no Serial Killer Days? If the economy is bad, then you get more hungry kids, more domestic violence, more thefts, more farm accidents because the farmer won't have as much money to keep his equipment up-to-date. There will be more *net* deaths. You can bank on that. Do we all want that on our conscience? Do we?"

19

Allrighty, gents and genteels, wasn't that the cutest thing you ever did see?" said emcee Wally Axel, popular deejay at KILU radio, after the Scream Queen contestants finished their "Who Will It Be?" opening number and danced offstage. "Aren't they just darlin'? I sure as heck wouldn't want to be a judge tonight. How could anybody pick just one?"

As soon as Debbie and the other young women left the sight of the audience, they hustled into the changing room to shed their leotards and throw on their gowns. Next on the program was the judges' questions, the most unpredictable event in the pageant. Not only were the contestants picked at random, but they did not know the content of the questions beforehand.

Most of the other girls were already lined up to return to the stage as Debbie slipped into her shoes. She gave her hair a quick brush and hurried to get in line. Standing in front of her was Molly Lovey, who looked back at Debbie and smiled pleasantly. "Gosh, this is all so exciting," she said.

Debbie smiled back at her. She hadn't had an opportunity yet to comprehend her rival's mysterious reappearance. Miss Exeter had acted like she fully expected Molly to show up at the last minute, making no comment other than telling her to hurry and get into formation. The other girls gave her odd looks, but followed their mentor's lead and pretended like nothing out of the ordinary had occurred.

"Very nice job," Miss Exeter said, joining them backstage. "You all looked like professionals out there. Now remember, don't step in front of Mr. Potz during 'Mr. Mayhem.' He is the star. The audience wants to see him. Make them believe he owns your hearts."

Soon their cue came and the contestants glided back into place, lining up in a row. A microphone stood forebodingly at the center of the stage, illuminated by a spotlight. Wally Axel waited beside the microphone, giving the girls a boyish grin, his capped teeth gleaming, the light bouncing off his shiny hairless pate.

"Well, well, look who's back!" he announced, batting his hands together. The crowd joined in. Waving at them to be quiet, he said, "Next up for our brave contestants is a question and answer session with our panel. Contestants will be judged on poise, personality, and the clarity and content of their answers." He removed a card from his tuxedo pocket. "First up is . . . Lois Langtry!"

The neophyte contestant got a horrified look on her face and stiffly walked up to the microphone. Judge Maynell Bell, award-winning beautician and massage therapist, gave Lois a genial smile and said, "Good evening, Miss Langtry."

"G-G-Good evening, ma'am."

"Here is your question: What is the closest you have ever come to getting murdered in your bed and how has it affected your hopes for world peace?"

Lois stood mutely for what seemed like an infinite moment, shifting her weight. Debbie felt sorry for her, sensing the panic that was in the newcomer's mind. Debbie recalled the first time she had been put under the gun. She had never forgotten the question: What is the biggest bruise you've ever had and how afraid were you when you first discovered it? Fortunately, her stammering, jumbled answer was lost forever.

"Well, the closest I've ever come to getting murdered in my bed," Lois began slowly, "was this one time, I woke up and felt something biting me on my arm. I slapped at it and it felt all wet.

I turned on the light and saw a big squashed mosquito on me. The blood was kind of splattered. It . . . it could have been carrying some kind of deadly disease or something. It made me appreciate how . . . er . . . the nations of the world need to get along and don't try to attack each other in the middle of the night, like mosquitoes do." Lois turned abruptly and found her place in line to a smattering of applause.

Ouch, Debbie thought. Maybe the presence of Kirk Potz threw her off.

"Thank you, Lois Langtry!" said Wally Axel. "A frightening story indeed!" He glanced at his card. "Next up is . . . Samantha Sink!"

Samantha confidently approached the microphone, her black gown flowing behind her like night grasses. Her years of competition really show, Debbie thought. I hope I look as poised as she does when it's my turn.

"Good evening, Miss Sink," said Gray Delaware, owner of Gray's Ammo Depot, located at 313 E. Main St.

"Good evening, sir," Samantha said with a slight curtsy.

"Your question is: Which weapon would you rather get killed with, a knife, a gun, or poi-son, and how would it help bring more freedom into the world?"

Without missing a beat, Samantha rattled off her answer. "If I had to choose, the weapon I would most prefer to get killed with would be a gun, preferably small caliber. But to tell you the truth, I would rather be stabbed first, *then* shot."

Utterances came from the audience. Is that delight or horror? Debbie wondered.

"It would bring more freedom into the world," Samantha explained, "because people who heard about it wouldn't know what to expect the next time. He could use the gun first, then the knife, or just the gun, or just the knife. More choices, more freedom. Thank you." Samantha crisply broke away from the spotlight and was swept back into line by an enthusiastic ovation.

Boy, she really did a good job, Debbie thought. That really puts the pressure on the rest of us. When a good performance is turned in so early, that raises the stakes in the judges' minds about what to expect from the performances that follow. Samantha was fortunate to get such an early draw.

"Our next lucky girl," said Wally Axel, "is . . . Debbie Morning!"

Debbie tried not to show any emotion as she left the security of her fellow contestants and found the spotlight. She glanced at Wally, who gestured to judges' row.

"Good evening, Miss Morning," said Gertrude True, director of nursing at Standard Springs Memorial Hospital.

"Good evening, ma'am," said Debbie.

"Your question tonight is this: What would it take to make you literally die of fear?"

Debbie blinked. Oh my gosh, she thought in a panic. What a horrible question. I have no idea what to say. *Die* of fear? I can't even make myself afraid enough to develop a rash. What would Samantha say? I can't fake it, they'll know. The spotlight suddenly felt hot on her face. Her throat became dry. She blinked again.

Judge True gazed at her expectantly.

Debbie's mind went fuzzy and numb. Her mouth refused to open; it was like trying to pry the lid off a jar of canned peaches. "I . . . I honestly must say that I don't know what it would take to make me die of fear. I think I'm pretty afraid right now, to tell you the truth, although probably the worst that could come out of it would be a nice little fainting spell. . . ."

No more words came into Debbie's mind. She backed away from the microphone, watching the crowd, who regarded her silently. A few hands patted together. Debbie looked for her family, but couldn't spot them. She turned suddenly and hurried back into place.

"Thank you for that unique perspective!" said Wally Axel, his voice booming through the gymnasium. "Now, our next big contestant to face our next big question is . . . Molly Lovey!"

Wild cheers rocked the joint.

Molly stepped into the spotlight, no sign of unsteadiness in her gait. She didn't wave or otherwise acknowledge the crowd in order to gain an advantage, and Debbie respected her for that.

"Good evening, Miss Lovey," said Wilhelmina Frougenfarmer, the druggist, obviously pleased at being the one to question the reigning champeen.

"Good evening, ma'am," Molly replied.

"The question for you tonight is this: What is the worst nightmare you ever had and how did it make you feel?"

"That's a very interesting question," said Molly. "As many of you know, I've been in the hospital, some type of coma is what the doctors say. But you don't know how it happened. Well, lately I've been having these dreams. I am in my house alone in the middle of the night and I am woken up by knocking on the front door, on the windows, all over the house. I can't see anything, there's just the knocking. I go to the front door, trembling, and I open it and look into the darkness and someone is out there, I know it, and I hear knocking on the other side of the house, and as I try to shut the door someone's pushing against it from outside, and I can't shut it and then the door swings open and the intruder is in the house with me and he says . . ."

The crowd leaned en masse toward the stage.

"HAPPY BIRTHDAY!"

The leaning didn't cease.

"Usually that's the point where I wake up and I'm left to imagine what happens next," Molly said, "but lately I haven't been waking up in time, and the other night, the night of my coma, the dream kept playing, too long, too long, and I saw and I felt what he did to me . . ." She told them, in great, graphic detail about the cake, the presents, the love, and so forth, right there as she stood in front of them, her small voice echoing hauntingly in the cavernous room.

The crowd gasped. Little kids began to cry.

Molly's head dipped, and she weaved slightly, then regained her balance. "That's all," she said, her breath coming in heaves. "Thank you."

The crowd didn't respond, whether unable or unwilling, Debbie was not sure. But she was sure she had never seen anything like it.

"Well, ah, er, thank you very much!" a confused-looking Wally the deejay said, attempting to recover from the unexpected path the pageant had suddenly veered onto. "This is certainly turning into a night of unusual, uh, events. Now for our next contestant . . ."

●

When the interrogations had concluded, the young women took their places on stage for the "Mr. Mayhem" number. Debbie knew she was trailing the pack at this point in the pageant, but it was still early. There was plenty of time to make up whatever ground she had lost. I'm not dead yet, she thought.

The stage went black.

A drumbeat started up, slow footsteps at first, then a trot, then a full chase. The first strains to "Mr. Mayhem" began. The spotlight flashed back on, shining on the center stage area, where Kirk Potz stood surrounded by the kneeling Scream Queen contestants, who clasped their hands together and gazed at Potz with affectionate dread.

Potz sneered at them.

Girls in the audience sighed and squealed.

"Well, they call me Mr. Mayhem," he crooned. "Mr. Mayhem, that's my name."

"That's my name," echoed the contestants.

"Oh, they call me Mr. Mayhem, Mr. Mayhem that's my name. If I don't commit some mayhem, I'm gonna hang my head in shame."

"In shame," cooed the backup singers.

The formation broke up and Kirk Potz spun away, swinging his hips and rapping his black boots on the stage. Suddenly he swiveled to face the girls again, who had lined up in a tight group perpendicular to the front of the stage.

"LET'S HAVE SOME MAYHEM!" Potz shouted, to the screams of his fans.

Kirk Potz made a thrusting motion with his forefinger at Tabby's chest. *"Well, I'm gonna do some stabbin'."* The girl threw her arms high and stylishly collapsed to the floor.

"Some shootin'." A handgun to the temple felled Samantha.

Debbie was next. She closed her eyes.

"Some chokin'." His hands were cold and he wasn't trying to be particularly gentle with her. She dropped to the floor and he released his grip.

"Some sluggin'." A dull thud sounded, and Debbie heard Molly grunt under her breath.

"Some lovin'." Debbie knew that Lois had lobbied Miss Exeter hard to be Kirk Potz's lovin' girl and she heard her drop to the floor with a thump, and then whimper some.

"Well, I said my name is Mr. Mayhem," sang Potz, careening into the final chorus, *"Mr. Mayhem 'til the day I die. If you ever run into me, you will surely find out why . . ."* He rode the final note a long time, the passion in his voice coming through strong. The ovation was deafening.

"Thank you!" Potz trumpeted. "You're beautiful!"

Debbie played dead until she heard the telltale rustle as the curtain was pulled shut. Then she opened her eyes and rolled to her feet, as did the other girls. Kirk Potz was gone. Lois, red-faced, got to her feet unsteadily, looking ready to swoon again at any moment. The contestants scurried off into the dressing room.

Next up was the talent competition. During the break Debbie kicked off her heels and found a towel, which she spread out on the floor in an unoccupied corner, and carefully sat down.

Miss Exeter came into the room, handing cups of water around, saying, "A very fine job. Mr. Potz told me as he left that you were the finest group of girls he has ever had a chance to work with, and believe me, he's worked with plenty."

"I thought he'd stay and hang out with us," Lois whined.

"He told me to tell you he would have liked to stick around, but he's a busy man, much in demand. I believe he said he still has to report in to his parole officer tonight." Miss Exeter cackled. "From the looks of you, Miss Langtry, I'm not sure you could have taken much more of Kirk Potz."

The other girls laughed, and Lois got even redder, although she giggled, too.

"Talent time is next," said the prison guard. "You know what order you're going on stage. Molly, you're going to have to go last, if you have no objections."

"No, ma'am, that's fine," she said.

Debbie gulped her water. Those stage lights were hot. She felt tired from all the excitement and stress.

"Mind if I sit down?"

"No, be my guest," Debbie said, scooting over. The other girl sat down beside her. They said nothing to one another for a minute, just sipping their water and cooling down.

"Boy, I think that Kirk Potz takes things a little too seriously," the resurrected Molly Lovey said, rubbing her cheek. "Do I have a bruise?"

"No," said Debbie. "A little redness maybe."

"I should have hit him back."

Lois, who was standing nearby, gave Debbie and Molly a dirty look and moved to the far end of the room.

"His hands were cold," Debbie added.

Her voice low, Molly said, "I didn't know you thought of me as your best friend."

"You saw the newspaper. . . ."

"My mom kept it right by my bed. When I woke up this afternoon it was the first thing I saw. That was very sweet of you to say, you know. I . . . I just didn't know you thought we were best friends. I mean, we hardly ever talked that much."

Debbie hesitated, then said, "To be honest with you, Molly, I'm not sure I said exactly what they said I did. But when the story came out, with my picture and everything, the other girls thought I was trying to pull something and they were mean to me and stuff. I know we never had much to do with each other, being rivals and everything."

"Is that why the other girls treat me the way they do, because I won the pageant and they haven't?"

"I guess so."

"But my mother said everyone came to visit me when I was in the hospital. She said you all came together and sat around my bed and prayed for my recovery and sang hymns. Why would you guys do that if you didn't like me?"

"I don't know about that," Debbie said. "I don't want to hurt your feelings. I wasn't with them if they did something like that. I came once by myself and sat with you for a while. That was the only time I was there."

"You came by yourself?"

Debbie nodded.

"Well, thank you for thinking of me. Did I look bad?"

"It was sad to see you like that," Debbie said. "Usually you have so much life in you. If I could have woken you up that second I would have. I told everybody I wanted you to get better. I didn't want to be in the contest if you weren't going to be there. It just wouldn't be the same."

"Are you sure you didn't say those things about me in the newspaper?" Molly asked her with a smile.

Debbie looked away self-consciously. She drained her cup and set it down by her leg. "That was a very interesting answer you had to your question," she said, wanting to change the subject. "You really dreamed those things?"

"Yes."

"Roger has been hearing your screams in the middle of the night. He thought you were just practicing."

"I wish that's all there was to it," Molly said. "I don't know what's going to happen when I go to sleep tonight; I don't know what my dreams will be. I feel like something is being drawn to me. Like I'm becoming the center of something, or maybe no longer the center. I almost feel . . . happy. What do you think that means, Deb?"

"I don't know. Something's up, though. Did you know they're thinking of changing the name of our town to Serial Killer?"

"No, I hadn't heard that. When did this happen?"

"I'm not sure. They're just talking about it right now."

"How could they not ask us?" Molly said. "We're the heart of this whole darn thing."

"Exactly."

Soon the talent program began, and Debbie was third to perform, so she got up to wait in the wings until it was her turn.

"Good luck," said Molly, lifting her paper cup in salute.

"Thanks."

Debbie walked carefully to the stage edge, trying not to make a sound, hidden by the curtains yet with a good view of the proceedings. Tabby had just left the stage, her face blackened by the powder burns. Samantha, dressed in a black leotard, reached center stage and announced formally, "I would like to present to you this evening an interpretative dance number. I am representing the spirit of Serial Killer Days. It is truth. It is symbol. It is the one who crawls through your window. Most of all, it is . . . fee-ear."

Samantha knelt down where she stood, curling up into a ball, her head tucked under her arms. The lights dimmed. The spotlight found her. She slowly spread her arms and brought her head up, rising at the same time, a forlorn expression on her face. She looked this way and that, then bounded across the stage, glancing over her shoulder with each step.

Golly, she's so graceful, Debbie thought.

After a somersault, a cartwheel, and a few spins, Samantha leapt into the air, her legs splayed out, landing slightly off balance. Then her eyes seemed to spot something. A look of terror. She waved her hands in front of her torso, backing up, step by step. Whirling, she ran up against an imaginary wall. Turning back, her mouth went wide and she screamed silently, rocking her body as the pretend blows struck her. She collapsed dramatically, and her legs shot straight up in the air, indicating death.

The lights went black. The crowd cheered.

A few seconds later the house lights flashed back on and Samantha bowed deeply twice, then waved to the audience and trotted off stage.

"That was a really nice dance, Samantha," Debbie told her competitor as she passed by.

She looked a little glum. "I landed wrong on one of my jumps," she said. "Did it look bad?"

"Hardly noticed it at all," said Debbie.

"That's a relief," Samantha replied, and headed to the dressing room.

Debbie nervously licked her lips, seeing Wally Axel take the microphone. "Isn't it amazing how much talent we have here in Standard Springs?" he said. "Isn't it? Isn't it?"

The audience applauded lustily.

"It reminds me of a joke I heard the other day . . ."

Some folks booed.

"Well now!" Wally said with mock offense. "Maybe we should let all the audience members decide this, eh? Okay, how many of you want to hear Wally Axel tell another joke?"

The reaction was decidedly mixed, Debbie thought, but Wally said, "Thank you for your show of support! You people in Standard Springs are the best!" Wally wiped the sweat from his upper lip. "Okay, here goes. Did I tell you folks I just got a new job? It's down at Lamprey's Lumber Yard. I'm in charge of spanking the knotty pine! Har, har, har."

The groans drowned out the handful of guffaws.

"Feel free to tell that one to your friends and neighbors," Wally said proudly. He glanced at a card in his hand. "Our next talented performer is . . . Debbie Morning! Debbie will be reading a poem for our pleasure tonight. I'm sure it will be a dandy one, too. Now let's have a nice hand for Debbie Morning!"

Debbie returned to the stage in a much less jumpy state than when she came out for the question and answer session. The words of Ole Rimbaud comforted and inspired her, and she was proud to share his slant on the world with her fellow Standard Springians. As Debbie clasped the microphone, the spotlight on her face, she thought she saw someone in a baseball cap and sunglasses standing in the aisle at the back of the gymnasium.

Was it him? She couldn't tell, although the thought that he

might be standing there in the shadows made her feel happy.

"The poem I'm about to read is very special to me," Debbie said. "It was written by Ole Rimbaud. I'd like to dedicate my reading tonight to him. It touched my heart and I hope it touches yours, too. It's called, 'Once, If I Recollect Right.'

"'Once, if I recollect right,'" she began, putting her whole soul into the words, "'my life was a Sunday dinner with all the fixins, where every heart said howdy, where every brewski flowed!'"

Debbie felt a warm glow fill her up inside. "'One night I gave Beauty a big ol' hug—and she didn't feel too swell, and I called her some sort of four-letter word. My hope has shriveled up like a prune. With a hop like a tomcat, I have caught and strangled every joy!'"

But she felt joy. Nothing but joy.

"'I will tear the curtains from every mystery—mysteries of religion or hog farmin' or what have you.

"'Hey, give me a thought from time to time. Can't rightly say I'd miss this world too much. My life was nothing but darn foolishness, too bad!'"

No, she thought, it's all too good.

"'We is out of the world, that's for darn sure. You can take that to the bank, oh you devil, oh you saint, oh you next of kin, oh the gosh darn soul rises, so does the bonfire . . .'"

Debbie had her arms out straight like a scarecrow, and now she slowly lowered them to her sides, and bowed her head, feeling the words vibrate down to her feet.

Hearty applause began, beginning in the rear of the gym, dwindling quickly as it reached the front rows. Debbie opened her eyes. The figure in the baseball cap she had spotted in the shadows was gone, if he was ever there at all.

She hurriedly left the stage, and saw that Molly was waiting in the wings, smiling from one end of her face to the other. Lois Langtry was there, too, her Adam's apple bobbing, a glazed look in her eyes, as Wally Axel said, "Blah, blah, blah, Lois Langtry!"

"You did so well!" Molly said in a hushed voice, taking Debbie's arm.

"Thanks," replied Debbie, as the pair went through the door to the dressing room, where the other contestants lounged about, Samantha combing her hair, Tabby throwing up in the corner. "The crowd didn't exactly go crazy," said Debbie. "At least that's the way it sounded."

"Oh, don't worry about the crowd," Molly said, giving Debbie a glass of water. "The judges don't pay much attention to that. Remember, they're sitting in the front, so they can't see the expressions of anyone in the room. They're concentrating on you, and believe me, you came across very much as a professional poetry reader."

"My teacher didn't want me to read poetry at all," said Debbie, sipping the water. "She thought it wouldn't wow the judges."

"Well, I can't speak for the judges," Molly said, "but it certainly looked to me like you held your own. You really put your heart in it. I think you'll be fine."

Debbie looked down. "So you're next to go, then."

"Oh, I still have a couple minutes. Do you want to sit again?"

"Sure."

They returned to their spot on the floor. One more hurdle, Debbie thought: the screaming. I'd better be in a good position going into that final event, because I'm sure not going to bring the house down with my screams. What if Mrs. Toddler is right? What if the judges think Ole Rimbaud is Mr. Nobody? Would even a passionate reading make a difference if they don't like him?

"Boy, you're really thinking, aren't you?"

"Sorry," Debbie said, brushing her hair back with her fingers. "I can't help it sometimes."

"I'm not making fun of you," said Molly. "What do you think about?"

Debbie looked at her carefully, glanced around the room, then returned her gaze to her rival. "Can you keep a secret?" she said quietly.

Molly nodded gravely.

"Ole Rimbaud is in Standard Springs," she whispered in Molly's ear. "I saw him this morning. I've always wanted to meet him.

He seems like such a nice person. He's sort of like my Kirk Potz."

"What's he doing in town?"

"Uh, he was in jail, actually."

"Jail? My gosh . . ."

"He just stole an apple from Mrs. Flatwire's orchard. But Molly, I thought I saw him in the back of the gym when I read my poem! Can you believe it?"

"That *is* something."

"I haven't told anybody this," Debbie said, "and Mr. Rimbaud made me promise not to tell anyone, so you have to keep this our secret, okay?"

"I won't tell anybody," said Molly. "I promise." She stood up. "I'd better get to the stage. It sounds like Lois is almost done."

Debbie wished her good luck and they shook hands. Debbie watched as Molly gathered up her long knives and headed through the door. When she heard her rival's name announced, Debbie went out to watch from the wings.

Molly began tap dancing to a catchy piano tune that Debbie had heard a million times before but she didn't know its name. She started flipping the knives into the air, first just one, its gleaming blade revolving crisply, the handle dropping squarely into her hand on the completion of its loop. Then two knives were airborne, and quickly three and four. And she didn't miss a tap.

Debbie squeezed her eyes shut. She had seen Molly perform this trick many times and it never gave her the feeling of anxiety she felt now. All she heard was the whup, whup, whup sound of the plastic handles hitting her palms, the rapping of her shoes on the stage.

This must be the longest tune in the world, Debbie thought.

Finally, the music ended and the crowd roared. Debbie opened her eyes to see Molly yanking a long knife from deep within her throat. She waved her knives above her head and grinned happily.

"Thank *you,* Molly Lovey!" Wally the deejay shouted. "Very frightening!"

Molly ran off stage.

"Gosh, I was really scared you'd get hurt," said Debbie.

"Oh, you shouldn't worry," Molly said. "I've been doing this since I was a baby, practically."

Following the talent competition there was a brief intermission before the screaming began. This gave the judges a chance to tally their marks, the audience a chance to get up and stretch, and the contestants a chance to muster up their fear. Wally Axel provided some entertainment with an off-key version of "Mac the Knife." Backstage the girls paced nervously, muffled shrieks in folded towels, forcing terror onto their smooth, young faces.

Debbie started warming up slowly, protective of her vocal chords, not wanting to risk straining them again at this late stage. She made low, growling noises at first, then raised her voice octave by octave until she could go no higher, still keeping the pitch low. Taking a towel, she pressed it against her mouth and did a couple of low-key screeches, then really released a full-fledged scream. She was pleased that her exertions had put no strain on her vocal chords. Her throat felt good and loose. She did some deep-breathing exercises, and noticed that Molly was sitting at a nearby table, a placid look on her face.

"Aren't . . . you . . . going to warm up?" Debbie asked, catching her breath. "We'll be going onstage in a few minutes." Then Debbie laughed, realizing her faux pas. "Isn't that funny, me telling you how to get ready for the screaming contest? Gosh, that's pretty silly of me. I don't know what I could have been thinking."

"No, it's okay," said Molly pleasantly, rubbing her palms. "I didn't take it the wrong way at all. Better than being ignored, that's for sure. How's your throat feeling?"

"Actually, not too bad. I just wish I felt the same things inside me as you do."

"Well, thanks. I guess I never thought of myself as being any different than you or anybody else."

"Okay, girls, attention!" Miss Exeter announced, clapping her hands at the center of the room. "This is the last event before the new Scream Queen will be crowned, so I want to take this opportunity to thank you for all your hard work these past few weeks. You've been one of the finest groups of girls I've had a chance to work with. Whoever wins the contest tonight, I know we'll all be proud of her and she'll make us all proud, too. I wish all of you good luck in the future, and if I run into any of you at PowPow somewhere down the line, I'll slip a file into your gruel."

The contestants gave Miss Exeter a nice hand and a slug on the arm before trooping out the stage door. A boisterous ovation greeted the girls as they reappeared on stage and assumed their positions. There was a piano off to the right edge of the stage. Most of the girls liked to use an accompanist, although a few preferred to scream a cappella, which was considered by longtime traditionalist pageant watchers to be a scandalous practice.

The first contestant to scream without accompaniment, Debbie recalled, was Felice Nettles, who some ten years ago stunned the audience by ushering her shocked and protesting pianist off the stage, and then returning for a solo scream. She was booed off the stage that night, but the next year two girls followed her lead, getting no boos but still awarded with bottom feeder finishes. By the third year there was a trio of soloists and they were no longer considered heretics and were judged fairly, even garnering a few cheers.

Legend built up around these pioneers to the point where it was difficult to distinguish fact from fiction. Debbie had been told by Mrs. Toddler that Felice Nettles's stunt wasn't as spontaneous as it initially seemed, that she had planned it all well ahead of time, and that the pianist was just putting on a big act. I should know, Mrs. Toddler had said, because *I* was the pianist.

"Here's the moment you've all been waiting for!" Wally Axel bellowed. "IT'S SCA-REAMIN' TIME!"

"YAH!" the crowd responded.

"You know the rules," said Wally. "A minute of pure, stark fear, and then we'll have us a new Scream Queen. The order of contestants was determined by lot before the pageant began. Please remember to hold your applause until all the contestants have finished screaming. Now, our first girl is . . . Lois Langtry!"

Boy, Lois sure got the short straw again, Debbie thought, as the rookie moved timidly to the microphone. Debbie was up last, which was good in some respects because then she could see exactly what she had to beat, but on the other hand, if someone totally killed, it would be hard to go that contestant one better, at least in the eyes of the judges.

Lois nodded at her pianist, who began knocking out a peppy ditty. Lois started to scream, her thin, reedy voice cracking. Debbie winced inside at her choice of music. It was much more effective, Debbie thought, to use a languid, somber selection rather than this carnival music. The music should accentuate the scream, bring out its finer points, not overshadow it and dictate how the audience will hear it. There's no space for that here, she thought. But for a first-timer this might be a good strategy; if her flaccid screams were hanging out there on their own, they would sound worse than they did now with a musical arrangement that distracted if not drowned out her voice. Perhaps as she matured, that would change. And perhaps the fear, which was absent tonight, would come as well.

"AAWEEEE! AAWEEEE!" screamed Lois.

She reached a crescendo, such as it was, then bowed and returned to her spot in line.

"Thank you, Miss Langtry!" Wally said. "We know we'll be hearing more from you in the years to come."

Samantha Sink was given the nod. She was an a cappella screamer and the moment her first shriek pierced the air in the gym, Debbie knew she would have her work cut out for her. The long, lingering screams seemed to be coming from deep within her soul. Her face was contorted in fear. It raised gooseflesh on Debbie's arms. Samantha paused, and Debbie figured she was done, but then she let loose another heartrending wail. She must have really done some conditioning, Debbie thought. She's improved a lot over the past year.

Children in the audience began crying, a sure sign of a successful program. Finally the screaming was over, and Samantha returned to the line, wearing a proud look.

Tabby Sorensen was up next, and did a decent job, although she was a notch below Samantha. Debbie grew anxious, knowing her time was approaching soon. She felt a big bead of sweat rolling down her cheek, and resisted the urge to wipe it away; nice touch, for a victim.

Next in line was Molly Lovey. Some unauthorized clapping broke out as she clasped the microphone. Wally Axel shot a disapproving glance at the offenders.

The accompanist began playing an appropriately morbid piece, and Debbie could practically see the audience bracing themselves for the onslaught that was about to ensue. The piano kept playing, and Molly kept standing still and silent at the microphone.

This is getting to be quite the introduction, Debbie thought. Maybe she has a froggie in her throat, or is about to sneeze or get sick or something.

But the music continued and the audience waited and Wally Axel and the piano player were giving the Queen nervous looks.

There!

Molly's arms slowly levitated from her sides, as if they were operating independently of their host. Her palms turned to face the audience, and she began to give them a good old-fashioned Scream Queen wave.

Suddenly blood began streaming from her hands, spattering as it struck the polished wooden floor.

Blood.

Gosh!

No one rushed to her aid, or called for a doctor. She just stood there and waved, bleeding for the town.

Debbie moved for her, but Molly abruptly broke away from the microphone and rushed off the stage, clutching her hands to her chest. As she went by, Debbie saw her face, and it wasn't the tears or anguish she expected. Her expression was flat, perhaps a little sad.

Debbie looked back at Samantha. The girl just shrugged.

"She should have saved that for the talent competition, whaddya think?" said Wally, sidestepping the puddle of blood as he returned to his place at center stage. The man was trying to sound upbeat, but Debbie thought he looked ready to fall over. "We'll see if we can bring her back later to take another stab at it, how 'bout that?"

The crowd clapped tentatively in approval.

"Our final Scream Queen contestant tonight is . . . Debbie Morning!" Wally announced. "Let 'er rip, Debbie!"

Debbie stepped up to the microphone. She was trying to concentrate on something, anything, fearful and her technique, all the long hours of practice, but Molly kept worrying her. What happened to her? What did it all mean? Stop thinking about her, you can talk to her later, you silly girl. This is the most important moment of your life. Debbie quieted the voices inside her and nodded at Mrs. Toddler, who smiled and began playing the familiar opening chords.

From out of the shadows she saw him come. He rushed down the center aisle to the front of the stage. He pulled something long and menacing from a coat pocket, unsheathed it, and held his left hand up, the back of the hand facing her, fingers splayed.

"Roger, no! . . ."

Then with a ferocious swipe he brought the knife down. The blood spurted and his pinky plopped to the floor.

"AAIIIIEIEIEEEE!" Debbie screamed. "AIIIIIEEEEEE! AIEEEEE!" She felt herself drift to the ground, and the last sound she heard was the bedlam, the shouts, the applause.

20

While a random act of violence to aid a contestant is not strictly prohibited by pageant rules, it's going to be difficult to tell how the judges will react," Debbie heard Mrs. Toddler say as she came to consciousness on a table in the dressing room.

Groggy, Debbie attempted to sit up, but firm hands forced her back down. "You had better rest for a bit before you try to go anywhere," Mrs. Toddler said, and Miss Exeter nodded in agreement, saying, "You've had a nasty shock, my dear."

"How . . . how did I get back here?" Debbie asked, trying to piece together the last few jumbled moments of her life. "I remember . . . Roger." She shut her eyes, trying to shoo the horrible image from her mind.

"You fainted and we carried you back here," Mrs. Toddler said.

"How long have I been out?"

"Just a few minutes," said Miss Exeter. "Wally Axel called for a short intermission so the judges can tally up the scores, and give you a chance to revive. Most people thought it was part of the program. You lay here for a couple minutes and then we'll see if you can make it back on stage for the announcement of the winner."

"The winner . . . ?"

"You have a chance," explained Mrs. Toddler, "because of the unprecedented nature of the situation. This is the most amazing thing that's happened in the pageant since Felice Nettles kicked me off stage and screamed solo. The judges may think it's the greatest thing they've ever seen or, on the other hand . . ."

"Roger, is Roger okay?"

"The boy was well prepared," Miss Exeter said admiringly. "He apparently was carrying a compress as well as ice to keep the pinky fresh. Doc Sellit says it'll be like sewing on a button, although you know how Doc likes to talk himself up."

"He was grinning as they carried him out of the gym," Mrs. Toddler said soothingly, with a comforting pat on Debbie's arm. "He'll be fine."

Debbie sat up slowly. Hands moved to restrain her, but she said, "I'm feeling all right now. Not dizzy at all hardly."

"Take your time," said Mrs. Toddler. "I'm sure Wally still has several hundred more bad jokes he'd like to tell."

With the aid of her mentors, Debbie planted her feet on the floor. She felt a little wobbly and lightheaded, but otherwise not too terrible, considering the circumstances.

"Are you sure you're well, dear?" Mrs. Toddler asked.

"I'm okay," Debbie said, nodding. "I feel okay." She looked around the room with concern. "Where's Molly?"

"I don't think Lovey has what it takes anymore," Miss Exeter said. "She made a mockery out of the pageant with her behavior tonight."

"Let's find out who the winner is," said Mrs. Toddler, taking Debbie's arm, "then you can go home and have a good night's sleep and by tomorrow morning none of this will seem like it ever happened at all."

Debbie pulled her arm free and headed for the door leading to the hallway.

"Not that way," Mrs. Toddler corrected her. "The stage door is over here."

"She must still not be herself," said Miss Exeter.

Turning to face them, Debbie said, "I'm not going back out on stage."

"But you might win," Mrs. Toddler protested. "You don't know what . . ."

"I'm sorry," Debbie said. "I have to leave now. Thanks for all your help, both of you." She smiled wanly and went out the door.

"But Debbie . . . !" Mrs. Toddler called out after her.

Debbie hurried down the empty hallway, the voices behind her fading. She cut down a side corridor, kicked off her heels, and pushed open the big blue door. The evening air was a relief after being under the hot lights all night. She wiggled her toes on the cool pavement. A June bug dragged itself across the sidewalk. She heard crickets, a train whistle in the distance. She soaked up the black sky, the white clouds crossing the face of the moon, the stars.

Going down the sidewalk outside the building, Debbie felt a funny feeling in her stomach, as if she was a kid who got lost on her way to school. The pageant had ended, for her. What would be taking its place? Would there be only emptiness to come? She felt a momentary impulse to race back onstage and tell the audience that everything was okay, and could we all please be normal again? Her legs felt like running. She longed for the approval of Mrs. Toddler and Miss Exeter. Passing by the tennis courts, she stopped at the edge of the playing field.

There was someone sitting in the middle of the field.

Debbie peered into the darkness. She started walking. The figure was clasping her knees, a dark gown falling to her ankles. She didn't move until Debbie was only a few feet away. She raised her head, and Debbie knelt down in front of her.

"So, did you win?" Molly asked, a sweetly sad expression on her moonlit face.

"Beats me," said Debbie. "I'm a truant, too."

Debbie told her what happened with Roger. "Well," Molly said evenly, "he must really care about you."

"I guess he does. I hope he doesn't mind that I skipped out."

"I'm sure he'll understand."

"So what the heck happened to you?" Debbie asked, plucking blades of grass and letting them slip between her fingers. "Are you feeling sick or something?"

"No, I'm fine," Molly said, showing her palms, now smooth and unstained. "I . . . I'm not exactly sure what happened. I heard my name and I got up to the microphone and everything seemed fine and I heard the music playing and . . . I don't know . . ."

"Were you scared?"

"Not scared. I don't know. I've never bled like *that* before. Gosh, I don't mean to sound so mysterious. Maybe there's a perfectly normal explanation for it. I just don't know what it is right now."

"You look different," Debbie said.

"I certainly don't feel like myself. I feel like somebody, though, and I wish I could find out her name."

"So here we are."

Molly nodded, smiling. "Here we are."

"I think I stirred up some mosquitoes when I came over here," said Debbie, standing up and brushing her hand down her arm. "Why don't we walk?"

"Great."

As they strolled through the field, heading for the sidewalk along the street, people began streaming out of the main entrance to the school. There were happy voices, laughter, the joyous screams of children. Debbie and Molly stopped and watched the celebration. Most of the activity seemed to be centered on one person in particular.

"Looks like Samantha is Queen," Molly observed.

"She did a good job," said Debbie. "She worked hard for it."

"I'm happy for her."

"Me, too."

They reached the sidewalk and started walking at a leisurely pace away from the school. Soon they were at the edge of the athletic field, the end of the school grounds, and now houses lined the sidewalk, warm yellow lights shining in the living rooms, blue television rays flashing on the white walls.

"What are you going to do now?" Debbie asked. "With your life, I mean."

"I was thinking of trying to get a job at the hospital, maybe be a nurse someday. I'm not sure. Either that or go to cosmetic school. What about you?"

"I guess I wasn't thinking of a career, really. I always figured I'd get married and be a mom and stuff."

"Roger?"

Debbie said nothing.

"There's certainly no hurry," Molly said. "That's my view. We're not that old."

"But to do such a thing, for me . . ."

"There's most certainly no hurry."

They had reached the end of the block. The street veered sharply downhill from where they stood. "Let's head back, okay?" Molly said.

"Sure."

The girls turned and started back to the school. As they walked, Debbie looked in the picture windows of the homes they passed. People were gathered around their televisions, talking, feeding birds in a cage. It's not really window peeping, she thought. I'm just walking down the street. I have to look at something, don't I?

Inside one house there was a larger-than-average television. On the screen were two heads with their mouths moving, a newscast from the looks of it. Above their heads, like a banner, was this word, written in red: DANGER.

"It's a beautiful night, isn't it?" said Debbie, and the two shadows laughed and strolled on through the darkness.

21

Arvid Morning woke up screaming.

He lay disoriented, gulping for air, sweat stinging his eyes. The body beside him stirred.

"Are you okay, dear? I heard something. . . ."

"I'm fine," he replied. "Everything's fine. Go back to sleep now."

"You're shaking," Mrs. Morning said, taking him in her arms. "It's all right, it's all right now."

"I . . . I had the dream again."

"Oh gosh. I was hoping you'd be done with it this year. I think that every year, every year I have such hopes. Was it the same as always?"

"Yes."

Yes, always the same. The big wind blows open his office door. The precious index cards fly from the board, spiral out the door, and down the street. He tries chasing them, but his legs feel like they are melting. Parade participants show up. Where do I go? What do I do? They mill about and then give up and wander off, leaving the director to march alone up the parade route, the gauntlet.

Without pants.

Arvid began to weep.

She stroked his head, held him tighter.

"I can't get rid of it," he said. "Every year it's the same. Every year I think it will be the last. I do a good job on the parade, don't I? We've had some problems, like the time the railroad crossing arm hit the band members on the head, but nothing major, never a disaster."

"You've always done a good job. You've done a lot for this town."

Arvid got out of bed and went to the window. The predawn sky was beginning to lighten, but the stars were still bright. Have I done everything right this year? he wondered. Is there anything I overlooked? Have to call the weather service this morning. Have to check the route one final time. Was that all? Could things really go so smoothly?

"It's just tension," his wife said. "We always forget how it is the day of the parade. You have more responsibility than anyone. It's perfectly natural that you have nightmares. They're anxiety dreams, that's all they are."

He said nothing.

"Why don't you come back to bed? You're going to need as much sleep as you can get. You have a long day ahead of you."

"I don't think I can sleep anymore. There's too much to do."

"You'll have plenty of time. You've been working so hard all week. You told me yourself yesterday that everything was in tip-top shape, didn't you?"

"I know, but I want to go over the lineup again. I'm thinking of moving the Shriners right behind the headquarters division. I'm afraid people's attention will flag if they stay in the second half of the parade. They should be highlighted. But if I move them up, there will be a gap later in the parade."

"Well, I think they're fine right where they are," Mrs. Morning offered. "You want to spread out the gunfire throughout the whole parade, don't you?"

"Yes, but I could use some of the more heavily armed clowns in their spot." He ran a hand through his hair, head down. "I don't know, maybe I should just stick with my instincts and not analyze things to death."

"I think that's a very good idea, dear."

Arvid returned to bed and tried to go back to sleep, but found himself seeing the parade in all its myriad details, worrying about everything from the screws on the historical society float to the semaphores on Main and Pain, hoping that he had calculated the clearances on all the floats correctly.

It's no use, he thought. He quietly climbed out of bed, dressed, and left the bedroom, carefully shutting the door behind him. As he went down the hall he peeked into Debbie's bedroom. She was asleep, one leg over the edge of the bed, covers strewn onto the floor. Poor kid, he thought. She had a tough night. But she hadn't seemed that upset about losing, which was good, a sign of maturity, perhaps.

Arvid nudged her door shut and headed downstairs.

After drinking a quick cup of coffee, Arvid left the house. The sun had just risen, and the streets on this Saturday morning were empty. He usually waited until late afternoon to tour the parade route, the later the better to spot last-minute problems, but there would be more traffic then. I can always do another run later in the day, he thought, getting into his car.

Arvid drove to the fairgrounds, the location of the marshaling area. Idling outside the gates, he could see the grounds were wet, although that was just morning dew. It was fortunate that there had been no heavy rains in the past week or two. In previous years they had not been so lucky, and the marshaling area had to be moved from the fairgrounds quagmire to the side streets adjacent to the parade route. This was not the worst alternative, but there was the greater likelihood of confusion among the units when they gathered on the side streets and weren't able to spread themselves out as much as they could at the fairgrounds.

Leaving the fairgrounds, Arvid took the designated side streets to Pain Lane, driving slowly, expertly scanning both sides of the street, the street itself, and the area overhead. The entire path from the fairgrounds to Pain checked out clear. He turned and started up Pain, heading toward Main Street and the heart of downtown Standard Springs.

About a block from Main, just short of First Street South, Arvid pulled to the curb. Frowning, he climbed out of the car and walked across the street. By the curb outside Wrisky Savings and Loan, he got down on his hands and knees and inspected the blacktop. There was a depression in the street, a pothole that had been filled, but not enough asphalt was used so the weight of the parked cars had created a smooth crater. Have to call the Sheriff's office and get a quick maintenance job done, he thought.

Arvid resumed his tour, passing Main and Pain, now on to the north end of the parade route. Things looked fine for a couple of blocks, but near the corner of Pain and Nordgren he discovered a parked car, no major problem under normal circumstances. However, this automobile was up on blocks, and had no tires. Going to need wheels before you can tow it, he thought, and made a mental note to make this obstruction his first priority.

The remainder of the route looked acceptable, as did the dispersal area off of Pain and Maple. Not too bad overall for six in the morning, he concluded. The problems he had found should easily be resolved by noon, which left over half a day until the parade began, and the opportunity to discover new problems.

Arvid spent the rest of the day in his midtown office making final adjustments to the schedule, fielding phone calls, making trips to the various float locations, helping their frantic designers with minor adjustments and foul-ups. He worked methodically, carefully, knowing any wrong decision now, no matter how small, would loom very large when it motored down the parade route before two or three thousand spectators.

By mid-evening, things seemed to be settling down, so Arvid walked to the Burgerama for dinner. They had their special menu in place; he ordered a Serial Killer Burger with cheese and a medium Fear Beer (which was really regular draft root beer tinged with blood-hued coloring).

After gobbling down his food, Arvid headed back to the office, stopping at the site of the mini-pothole. He was pleased to see that the city crews had already refilled the depression. He stepped on it to make sure and got a nice coating of fresh tar on the sole of his shoe for his trouble.

Arvid was always amazed at how people pitched in to help each other during Serial Killer Days. Tasks that took weeks or months to complete during every other part of the year were resolved in minutes during the third week in July. Arvid thought of the pothole outside his own house, which had been menacing his family since early spring. Even with his stature in town he was unable to make the wheels of city hall roll in his direction. Maybe I could divert the parade route to go past my house, he thought with bemusement.

As he walked back up to Main and Pain, he saw that the Pequin sisters had already staked out their spot on the parade route, setting their lawn chairs and coolers at the stop lights in front of Frougenfarmer's Drug Store.

"Evenin', Merta, Gerta. Nice night for a parade, eh?"

"Couldn't ask for a nicer night," said Gerta, who was usually identical to Merta except she wore a red stocking cap all year round.

"Just lovely," echoed Merta.

"Any Shriners this year?" inquired Gerta.

"Why, of course," said Arvid. "Couldn't have a proper parade without them."

"How about animals?" Gerta asked. "I like animals."

"Oh, there will be a good share of animals. Plenty of horses. Do you like horses?"

"Horses are fine," said Gerta. "How about monkeys?"

Arvid stroked his chin. "Hmm, not so sure how we're set in the monkey department. I don't believe there are any, although I'd have to double-check to make sure. We could always have a last-minute entry, of course."

"Oh, that's okay," Gerta said, with a wave of her twisted hand. "There's more to life than monkeys, you know."

"Not so many clowns, I hope," Merta suggested.

"You don't like clowns?" Arvid asked.

"She's scared of them," Gerta explained. "They're okay by me, although I must say I very possibly would not invite one into my home."

"Into our home!" Merta exclaimed with a shiver.

"Well, there will be some clowns, and I can guarantee you they will all be very well-mannered. You let me know if they aren't."

"I will!" said Merta.

"Have a good time, ladies," said Arvid. "Feel free to stop in at my office next week and tell me what you thought of the parade."

"Oh, we always love it," said Merta.

"We surely do," agreed Gerta.

They are the true heart of Serial Killer Days, Arvid thought as he left them. He went back to his office, locked the door, and stared at the index cards on the wall for a few minutes. Then he switched off the lights, got down on his knees in the middle of the carpeted floor, and prayed for some time.

●

Just after eleven o'clock Arvid packed a stack of master marshaling diagrams, a box of walkie-talkies, a pair of bullhorns, and other tools of the trade into the trunk of his car and drove to the fairgrounds. It was odd to see the streets so busy at this late hour; various parade units rolling down the shadowy side streets, kids on bikes, the dark refreshment stands. When he arrived at the grounds he saw that most of the committee members were already present, standing in the staging area, which was lit by field lights. Franklin Wrisky Jr. was there, as was Mary Beth Jo Raisin and her sons, Buzz and Jerry, and Deputy Dan, and a couple of the ladies from the sausage plant.

"Hello folks," he said, passing out a diagram to each of them. "Here's our updated master list. Mary Beth Jo will be manning the front gate, and directing the units to their proper areas. Just make sure they belong in your area and keep a good distance between units, because some of them might need room to turn around."

"What about no-shows?" a sausage lady asked.

"We'll give them as long as possible to show up," said Arvid. "When you hear the first warning signal, call me right away and let me know who's missing, and I'll try to determine if they're late or not able to make it at all. If any unit is not here by the time we pull out, close up the gap as best you can."

"Gotcha," she said.

"Deputy, it looks like you've blocked off the adjacent streets already," Arvid said.

"Yes, sir."

"Keep an eye out for interlopers. Kids are drawn here like you wouldn't believe. For their own safety we need to keep the grounds secure."

"I'll take care of it," said the Deputy.

Arvid handed out the walkie-talkies. "Franklin, if any of the units in the headquarters division doesn't arrive by one, let me know. I expect them all to be here, barring a flat tire or something else unforeseen. I inspected all the headquarters units earlier today, and they all checked out, except for the bands, of course."

"Right."

"Speaking of bands," Mary Beth Jo said, pointing to the gate.

The orange school bus chugged through the fairgrounds gate and rolled across the field. Deputy Dan flagged them down, waving them to the parking area by the sheep barn. The band members piled out, an impressive sight in their identical black uniforms with pale faces and dark green grease paint beneath their eyes. They were lugging their instruments and a variety of weaponry, from shotguns to swords, each reflecting the individual's personality.

Arvid walked over to them and shook the hand of Golbyville's long-time band director, Moe Greel, his uniform bedecked with gold tassels and ammo clips.

"How are you doing, sir?" Arvid said.

"Couldn't be better," said Greel. "The kids are really up tonight. They'll put on a good show." He winked, rubbing his fingers together. "Thanks for the extra, you know."

"You're the best band in the county," said Arvid. "I'm glad we could work something out."

Arvid directed the band down to where Franklin was now situated. Other units began to arrive at the gate, the dark floats, the morbid clowns. Arvid scaled the wooden tower, which was actually the judging stand for the horse shows at fair time. From here he could get a panoramic view of the grounds and head off any problems before they turned into catastrophes.

The Shriners' trailer arrived, hauling their little black cars; and as they unloaded the vehicles, Arvid still had second thoughts about not moving them up to the headquarters division. It's still bothering me, he mused, so there must be some tangible problem here.

Arvid switched on his walkie-talkie. "Tower to third sector, over. Can you read me, Mary Beth Jo?"

"Not too loud but clear."

"I've got a change for you. Tell the Shriners they're up in the headquarters division, the final unit in the division. I'm sure they won't mind. In fact, I think they'll be thrilled. Over."

"Will do. Any problems? Over."

"Nope. Just the chairman's gut feeling. I'll let Franklin know what's coming his way. Over and out." He waved at her, and she flapped her hand back at him.

"Tower to headquarters division. Over."

"Headquarters division here. Over."

"Franklin, I'm sending the Shriners your way. Put them at the end of the division. Let me know if you need more space. Over."

"Shriners at the end of the division. Should be plenty of room. Over."

"Thank you, Franklin. Over and out."

"You betcha. Over and out."

Coming through the gate, Arvid saw, was the Scream Queen float, towed by a pickup truck whose bed was filled with girls in black gowns. Arvid climbed down from the tower and wound his way through the clusters of floats and performers.

"Wrap the duct tape around your *ankles,* dear, not your knees."

"Hey, anybody seen my gun?"

"If you don't pick at it, Jimmy, it won't bleed."

"When is the Man in the Cage gonna get here?"

Reaching the headquarters area, Arvid saw that the girls were milling around the Scream Queen float, preparing to board. The float was covered in black flowers and red tassels and bunting and foil and blinking lights and blood. There were places for all the contestants to stand, leading up to the cage, which was unoccupied presently, and topped by an electric chair throne where the Queen herself would be seated.

"You girls did a fine job," Arvid said, as they noticed his arrival. "One of the best Scream Queen floats ever, in my professional opinion."

"Thanks, Dad," said Debbie.

"Samantha, you be careful up on top. Try not to move around too much. One year a Queen stepped onto the papier-mâché and sunk down into the float up to her neck. All people could see was her gloved hand, waving for help. They waved back, of course."

"I'll be careful," she said.

The Queen and her court scaled the float just as the Sheriff's car came through the gate, red lights flashing. Stopping the car alongside the float, the Sheriff got out and opened the back door, hauling out a dark-haired man in a pumpkin orange prison jumpsuit and handcuffs. People in the vicinity stopped what they were doing and gaped at him. He appeared docile at first, shuffling along with his head down as Sheriff Eeha led him to the base of the float, then the man suddenly raised his head and growled at the onlookers, his teeth bared, his eyes manic.

Everyone jumped back in alarm. Someone screamed. The Sheriff got him under control and prodded him up onto the float.

Arvid smiled and headed back to the tower, feeling more happy than he had for days.

22

Debbie Morning thought she must be dreaming.

As she was finding her place on the Scream Queen float, a small platform on the left side just below the cage, a car with a cherry on top drove up and out popped the Sheriff and his prisoner. She stared and stared and she couldn't believe it was him.

"Ole?" she said under her breath.

The man kept his head lowered, scuffing along to the float, wrists in bracelets. Suddenly he leapt at the bystanders, snarling and spitting. They retreated in fear. Someone screamed. Even Debbie flinched.

The Sheriff grabbed the prisoner by the collar and poked him in the back with his nightstick, forcing him up onto the front of the float, then following him as they ascended. The girls cowered as they passed by, and Debbie kept looking at Ole, but when he got to the cage he did not acknowledge her. Opening the cage door, the Sheriff prodded the man inside, then slammed the door shut and removed the prisoner's handcuffs. The Sheriff climbed down from the float, leaving the prisoner with the Queen and her court.

"Wow, he's a scary-looking one," said Molly, who was standing on the platform just in front of Debbie.

As the prisoner gripped the bars at the front of the cage and gazed out at the night with fierce eyes, Debbie said, "Yeah."

"I wonder how many he's killed?"

"I wonder . . ." Debbie said quietly.

Soon the novelty wore off and the onlookers wandered away from the cage and returned to whatever they had been doing. Debbie glanced up at Ole from time to time, not sure if she should try to get his attention. She was positive that he was putting on an act—well, maybe not positive but pretty sure anyway.

It was a question of which faith would be shattered. From the time she was a little kid through her first ride on the Scream Queen float, Debbie believed in the legend of the Man in the Cage. Everybody knew he was a bad man who had committed unspeakable acts against his fellow man. Of course, no one knew *exactly* what his crimes were, they were not spelled out in the souvenir programs, but rumors ran crazy during and after the Parade of Fear, and the town collectively chose which of the stories they found most to their taste.

Last year, for instance, the Man in the Cage had butchered a baby-sitter over in Hirsute County. Came right in the window while she was watching television, an old Roy Rogers movie. Didn't even wake the baby, which afforded him a spoonful of sympathy in some circles. In other years Standard Springs was treated to an arsonist, an axe murderer, and a standard issue cannibal. Debbie had never even considered questioning the reality of their alleged acts.

So if Ole was just playacting, then that meant that all the other men in the cage could have been pretending, too!

Debbie's mind boggled at the idea. Could such a thing be? Wouldn't her dad have told her?

Well, she thought, they didn't clue me in about Santa Claus until I was in junior high, so why should this be any different? What *else* haven't they told me? Maybe there is no such thing at all as a serial killer who visits Standard Springs every July. But that's silly. Someone *was* killed at the end of every Serial Killer Days. She knew that for a fact; she had seen them cart out the bodies. Okay, that was good, a solid fact around which she could build her new view of the world.

Now, was there any possibility that Ole was a killer? I haven't really known him for that long, she thought, at least on a face-to-face basis. I've known him through his poems for some time, though, and he's no murderer although he does write about rotted stuff a lot. Gosh, who can tell about people these days?

Debbie glanced at him again. Not my Ole! Not that sweet, sad face.

The bullhorn bleated, a first warning.

I should ask him right now; he'd tell me if he was a killer. Then she thought better of it. If I ask him here, now, then everybody will hear. Boy, would *that* ever be embarrassing. Maybe it would be better if I waited, go along with the act, if that's what it is. Or maybe . . .

"Hey, pumpkin."

Broken out of her reverie, Debbie turned and saw that Roger had arrived. As part of the cast of *The Sound of Maniacs,* he was in costume with the other members of the troupe, following in the slot behind the Scream Queen float. She visited him at the hospital earlier that day, but he was too sedated to recognize her.

"Hi," she said, looking at his heavily bandaged hand. "I wasn't sure if you were going to be able to make it or not."

"Aw, it was nothin'," he said, holding up his hand. "Doc didn't want me to come, but I figure there will be plenty of time to recuperate after tonight."

"Please don't hurt yourself: It's going to be a long walk for someone in your condition."

"I'll be okay," he said, and then got a serious expression on his face. "You know, it's okay that you didn't win. I caught your scream, or most of it anyway. People are sayin' it's the best scream this town has ever heard."

"Thanks. If I would have gotten a better question, I might have had a chance. Samantha really did a good job. She's improved a lot since last year."

He leaned in close and whispered, "With Molly out of it I

thought we were in for sure. What the heck happened to her anyway? Have you talked to her?"

"I'm not sure she knows," Debbie said carefully. "I think she just had enough."

He nodded. "Yeah, it's a lot of pressure, I suppose, to be someone so important, representin' your town to the world and all."

"That's not what . . ." Debbie began saying, but then the bullhorn tooted again. The caravan began moving, the float rocking as it rolled across the grass, the band ahead of them marching at a measured pace, heading toward the front gate.

"Gotta run," the boyfriend said. "See you later."

"Good-bye, Roger."

Molly looked back over her shoulder. "He was talking about me, wasn't he?"

Debbie nodded. Their eyes didn't break.

"What did you tell him?"

"Nothing at all."

Now that they were on the move, crawling down the side streets, making their way to Pain Lane, Debbie felt more at ease. The bands hadn't begun to play, the clowns were showing restraint, and the Shriners had not yet cut loose.

Debbie looked at Ole again. He still held the bars in a death grip, his jaw thrust out, his eyes focused on his next victim.

"Hey, Ole!" Debbie whispered up at him, cupping her hands around her mouth.

He turned his head slightly, still looking forward, and winked.

"I know you aren't a killer," she said. "I never doubted you for a minute."

Molly looked back with surprise. "That's your poet friend?"

"Yeah, isn't he something? Isn't he the cutest thing?"

The ears of the Man in the Cage turned a violent shade of red.

"I saw you in the back of the gym last night," Debbie said. "It was you, wasn't it? Did you like how I read your poem? That's okay, I know you can't answer now, but I figure you probably did. I like many of your poems, but of all of them that is probably the one I like best at the moment. I'd like to hear you read it some time. I'd really like that. Oh, don't try to answer now. We can talk after the parade, can't we? There's somewhere I'd like to take you."

The float cruised down the dark streets. In the distance Debbie could see the crowds lining the curbs at the start of the parade route. She began to feel a little excited and nervous. She didn't know how people would react to her, and especially to Molly. Would they jeer or boo? Would they throw things? Well, I'll boo right back at them, she decided with determination. We are the heart of this darn thing, and how we handle ourselves is our business. If they think it's so easy to stand up before a thousand people and scream your head off, well, then let them try it.

"I'm sort of nervous about this," Molly said, looking back, the sound of the crowd reaching them. "I don't want them to hate me."

"They won't hate you," Debbie reassured her. "You've done too much for this town. I mean, gosh, how many trips have you taken around the state to promote our town?"

"A hundred, probably."

"And you didn't get paid anything for it. You did it because you cared about the town, right?"

"Well, I took that responsibility when I accepted the title."

"So don't worry. Anybody who treats you like you did something wrong is just a big dumbhead, okay?"

"Okay."

About a block from the parade route the band broke into a high-stepping version of "The Funeral March," a clown flipped an executioner's hood over its head and kicked the heels of its big floppy red shoes, the lights on the Scream Queen float began winking, Ole began rocking back and forth in his cage, and a chorus of low moans became the melody of a summer night.

The job for the Scream Queens was to look afraid and cower; no one told them this, no one trained them, it was simply accepted as the way things were done, a tradition passed on from one year to the next.

However, as they slowly rounded the corner and maneuvered

up Pain Lane, and the murmurs of the crowd changed into cheers, Debbie told herself she would not blindly do something she did not feel, but then decided she still felt some sense of obligation to the pageant and the other girls. I'll just cower a little bit, she thought.

As they rolled down the first stretch of the parade route, Molly glanced back at Debbie. Her face was solemn. Something needed to be said, but Debbie could not find the words.

The parade was in full fear. The cheers changed to screams. Blood was running in the streets. The night was alive.

Debbie looked at faces in the crowd, hoping to spot someone familiar, but they were all strangers to her. She focused on the road ahead, forgetting about cowering, about the crowd, about everything.

"Hey! Ouch! What the heck! . . ." shouted a voice from above.

The outburst, Debbie saw as she turned her attention to the summit of the float, came from the new Scream Queen. Samantha was on her feet, a pained expression on her face, looking intently at the seat of the electric chair.

"What's wrong, Samantha?" Debbie asked.

"I got a shock!" she said in disbelief. "I was going to sit down, and then I did and . . . and . . ."

Molly looked back. "What happened?"

"Samantha said she got a shock," said Debbie.

"My gosh," Molly said, putting her hand to her mouth. "How did that happen?"

"I think somebody doesn't want me to be Scream Queen," said Samantha, on the verge of tears.

"What do you mean?" Debbie said.

"I mean somebody did something to my throne so I'd get electrocuted. That's what I mean. And I think it was a dirty, awful, rotten trick!"

"Are you saying one of *us* did it?" Debbie asked.

"What did she say?" Molly asked.

"One of us fixed her chair so it'd electrocute her!"

"Oh gosh, who would do such a thing?" said Molly.

Lois Langtry, stationed directly opposite from Molly on the right side of the float, looked over and asked what happened. Molly told her.

"Are you goofy, Samantha?" Lois yelled.

"Well, somebody did it," she said. "One of you must be jealous of me, that's all there is to it."

"That's really terrible of you," said Tabby, stationed opposite Debbie. "How could you think that of us?"

"Yeah," Lois chimed in. "I thought we were all friends."

"It really hurt!" Samantha said.

"There's the Deputy," said Molly, pointing to the side of the road, where Deputy Dan was confiscating a fluorescent green squirt gun from the occupant of a baby stroller. "Maybe he can help us."

"Good idea," Debbie said. She waved at the Deputy to come over. He gave the offender a stern look and trotted to their float, walking along to keep pace. "We have a problem," she told him.

"A problem? Okay, wait." He removed a notepad and stubby pencil from his tan shirt pocket. "I'm ready."

"It's Samantha. She says she got electrocuted when she tried to sit down on her throne. I didn't see it happen, but she yelped pretty good. She thinks one of us did it, but I think that's plain silly."

"Tell me the names of the suspects, young lady," he said, lips tight.

"Couldn't you just call my dad? Maybe there's something wrong with the float. He's on the route somewhere, I'm sure."

The Deputy looked at her for a long moment, then put his notepad away and unclipped the walkie-talkie from his belt. "This is Deputy Dan calling Director Morning," he said. "Are you there, Mr. Morning?"

The device squawked, and then her dad's voice came over, saying, "Morning here, Deputy. What can I do for you? Over."

"There's a problem on the Scream Queen float. Somebody got a shock. I'm on the scene conducting an investigation, but you might want to take a look yourself. Over."

"I'm on my way. Over and out."

In less than a minute a golf cart zipped up to the float, dropping off Arvid Morning, his pale red Serial Killer Days T-shirt already soaked in sweat. He ran up to the front end and spoke to the driver, then came back and said, "What's all this I hear about electrocution?"

Debbie told him what happened. He yelled up at the Queen, "Samantha, you all right?"

"I think I am. I don't know how someone is supposed to feel after they get electrocuted, though."

Mr. Morning scaled the float, keen eyes searching for a problem. He poked and jabbed at the throne, with a pencil and his finger, then removed a thin flashlight from his pocket and climbed down into the infrastructure of the float. A few minutes later his head reappeared, and he pulled himself back up onto the float.

"Attention, girls!" he called out. "Do not sit down! Repeat, do not sit down! We have a short circuit in the float. The foil shell is charged with electricity, so every time you touch it you will get a shock like Samantha did. Just stay put. It doesn't appear to be a major problem; we can get an electrician to fix it in a matter of minutes. But please stay where you are and there shouldn't be any more difficulties." He carefully descended from the heights of the float and hopped down onto the pavement.

"Thanks, Dad," said Debbie.

"That was quick thinking on your part, child." He jumped back into the golf cart and scooted away.

"What do you have to say now, Samantha?" Tabby yelled.

"Yeah, what about that?" Lois shouted.

"Now all of a sudden you're Miss Stuck Up," Tabby continued hotly. "Just because you won the darn pageant, now you think you're better than the rest of us."

"I don't think that at all!" Samantha protested, a panicky look on her face. "How was I to know it was a short circuit? I never worked with electricity before, I took home ec. You can't expect me to know that. I didn't mean it, guys. I really didn't!"

"Molly would never have thought something terrible like that about us," Lois called out.

"But, but . . ." said Samantha.

"Yeah, Molly would have trusted us," Tabby said. "We were all friends; it didn't matter if she was Queen or not. She never acted like she was better than us, she was just part of the gang."

"*I* always liked her," said the Man in the Cage.

Debbie gaped at Ole and laughed, then looked at Molly, who was gazing dutifully at the crowd, although Debbie could see the side of her face, which wore a broad grin.

"You've suddenly become Miss Popularity," Debbie told her.

Glancing back, Molly said, "I never knew I had so many friends."

"You better stop smiling," said Debbie, as the crowd began giving them disapproving looks, "or people will think something's wrong."

23

It's two A.M., folks, and if you don't know where your kids are, they're probably here at the annual Parade of Fear! This is Wally Axel, KILU radio, the voice of the friendly farmland, welcoming you back to our live broadcast at the corner of Main and Pain on this, the last night of Serial Killer Days. We'll be here all night so stop by and get yourself a free KILU bumper sticker and a free glass of ice water, compliments of the Standard Springs American Legion, where every Tuesday you can chow down at their all-you-can-eat taco feed.

"Passing by our location right now is the Scream Queen float. Its title this year is, 'Oh My God, What Are You Going to Do with That Knife?' A more frightened group of girls you'd be hard pressed to find. Just last night the new Scream Queen was crowned, Samantha Sink, daughter of Elmer and Delores Sink. Samantha is a junior at Standard Springs High School. Her favorite subjects are math, gym, and home ec. Her hobbies include softball, crocheting, and cowering in fear. I had the pleasure of emceeing the pageant and let me tell you that Samantha is one of the finest screamers this town has ever seen.

"This year's Man in the Cage is a scary character, let me tell you. I sure wouldn't want to see him in my dark backseat. Now don't spread this around, folks, but I heard that he murdered a homemaker over in Pale County. She was fixing dinner. Chicken-fried steak, I believe. He used a meat tenderizer, yes indeed. Don't want to tell you what *he* had for dinner.

"Next up we have the cast from *The Sound of Maniacs*. Sven Lagoon starred in this production as Hans, with Genevieve Gossamer as the lunatic governess. Hope you had a chance to get down to the high school and see it. It's hard to believe how much talent is in this town.

"Oh! Oh! Here they come! It's the famous Drive-By Shriners! They're doing their intricate figure-eight maneuvers and now they're sticking guns out the windows and firing on the spectators, who are taking it in good spirits, of course. Don't shoot, don't shoot! Ha, ha. Now the Shriners are peeling rubber, making their getaway to find their next victims, and there's a nice round of applause for them. Hey, it wouldn't be a real Parade of Fear without them, now, would it?

"While we're waiting for the next float to pass our way, folks, let me take this opportunity to say a word about one of our fine sponsors, Hamp's Hardware, located in the heart of downtown Standard Springs. Hamp's has a full line of chain saws, ball peen hammers, and duct tape. That's Hamp's Hardware, uptown selection at small-town prices. Tell 'em Wally Axel sent you.

"Here comes our next float, The Dark Refrigerator, sponsored by Lockwell's Appliance, Two Twenty-nine West Main. Featured is a twenty-foot-high papier-mâché replica of a refrigerator, complete with a door that swings open and shuts again. Riding atop the fridge is Miss Cold Storage, Vicki Kelver, a sophomore at Nodal High School. The theme for this year's float is: 'You'd Be Surprised at What You Can Fit Inside a Lockwell Refrigerator.' From my vantage point I can see a heart, a kidney, what looks like part of an arm, and what's that there, a spleen? Isn't that a spleen, Johnny? I'm asking my engineer, Johnny Sparks. No, here, use the microphone."

"Sure looks like a spleen to me, Wally."

"A spleen it is, then. Thanks, Johnny. He does a heckuva job keeping us on the air, folks. One of the many unsung heroes of the Parade of Fear. How many years have you been working for KILU, Johnny?"

"More than I care to remember!"

"Ho, ho, a real wise guy, that Johnny. Now you'd better get back to work before we're off the air for good!

"Oh, now you're in for a treat, folks. The sound you hear is the snappy cadence of the Campville Cow Bone Band. The members of the band are all farmers from Campville County, playing bones from cattle found in their own pastures. They've been a fixture at the Parade of Fear for many years and they always do a fine job. Play those cow bones, boys!

"Here's a treat for the kiddies! It's the Anti Claus float, with every kid's worst nightmare, the Anti Claus. Don't run screaming, kids, it's just a mechanical simulation. There at the back of the float you can see the Anti Claus in his workshop, sharpening something or other. He has no little helpers; the Anti Claus is quite the troubled loner, you see. In the middle of the float is the Anti Claus climbing through a dark bedroom window. Wouldn't want to be in those folks' shoes! At the front of the float is . . . well, I'd like to describe it for you, but the station has rules against that sort of thing. You'll have to come next year and see for yourself!

"Deputy Dan of the Standard Springs Sheriff's Department is walking by our booth and we'll see if . . . Deputy, could we have a word with you? It'll only take a minute. Just speak into the microphone, please."

"Well, just for a minute. I'm on duty, you know."

"And it's a fine job you're doing, Deputy. Now, Deputy, what sort of problems do you run into as a law enforcement officer at a parade like this?"

"The crowds are very well behaved, Wally. Lost kids are a problem. You see them wandering through the darkness and it's kind of sad. There's not much we can do for them."

"Good to hear! You really make a sacrifice, you men in uniform. You don't even get to see the parade, right?"

"That's right, Wally. I have to concentrate on my job. I get a great deal of satisfaction from that. Can I say something here, Wally?"

"You go right ahead, Deputy."

"I just want to tell folks to stay tuned to their radios because they're going to be in for a nice surprise come morning."

"Sounds pretty mysterious, Deputy, although I can't complain about the plug for the station. Is there anything more you can tell us about this surprise?"

"Not really, Wally. All I can say is that a new day will dawn in Standard Springs on Sunday morning. Now don't try to pry any more information out of me because it won't work. I am a trained law enforcement officer, you know."

"I would attempt nothing of the kind, Deputy. I learned to respect the badge way back when I was just a little tadpole."

"I know people maybe think the Sheriff's office is not doing its job because . . . well, you know there's this fellow running around town trying to take advantage of the situation for his own political gain. . . ."

"You're not talking about Rodney Owl, are you?"

"As a matter of fact, I am. He has shown . . ."

"There he is now, Rodney Owl, riding blindfolded on a unicycle that has a sign saying STANDARD SPRINGS SHERIFF'S DEPARTMENT! Rodney, get over here, there's someone who wants to talk to you! You don't mind, do you, Deputy?"

"Mind? There's a thing or two I'd like to tell him, man to man."

"Right over here, Rodney, follow my voice. Why don't you take your blindfold off? Turn your siren off, too. That's better. Now Rodney, the Deputy here has been taking your name in vain, so I thought it was only fair that you got equal time."

"Hey, folks, this is Rodney Owl. I'm getting down on my knees to ask you for your vote this fall. Standard Springs, Don't Throw in the Towel, Vote for Rodney Owl. That's all I got to say."

"You stop telling people we can't do our jobs! What do you know about being an officer of the law, huh? You aren't even qualified to be dogcatcher!"

"Hey, Deputy, if your department was in charge of dog catching, we'd be up to our clavicles in cocker spaniels!"

"Oh yeah? Oh yeah? Well, we'll see how smart you are tomorrow morning! Let's see how smart you are then!"

"What's tomorrow morning? Your sheriff having a retirement party?"

"While you've been out jabbering, we've been doing detective work. You won't have to worry about passing out any more buttons after tomorrow, you can count on that, buster."

"We've heard this all before, haven't we, folks? What exactly have you detected, Deputy? Go ahead, we're all listening."

"I'll tell you what I said before. There'll be a new day dawning in Standard Springs come Sunday morning. A new day."

"Yeah, it'll be a new day, all right. We'll have to change the signs from 'Standard Springs, Population 4,317' to 'Standard Springs, Population 4,316.' "

"You don't know nothing. You're a big blowhard."

"Talk, talk, talk, that's all we get from our Sheriff's Department. All talk. Yak, yak, yak, yak."

"All talk, huh? You'll see, Rodney Owl, you'll see!"

"Okay, fellas, thank you for that, uh, spirited exchange, but we've got a parade to cover! The blood is running in the streets, I can hear gunfire in the distance, and all in all it looks like we've got another humdinger of a Parade of Fear! . . ."

24

A new day, Deputy Dan thought, turning his attention again to the parade, leaving Wally Axel and that troublemaker Rodney Owl behind. It's been a long time since Standard Springs has seen a new day. He could barely remember a summer when there wasn't a serial killer on everyone's mind. It was a vague memory, almost dreamlike, those summers before the serial killer.

Deputy Dan smiled, leaving the darkness for a moment, pulling the memories close to his heart. Those long, hot days lasted forever, and even then he felt a want for more. He remembered riding his bike to Lake Tonto, spending the whole day fishing for bullheads. In the evening there would always be games to play, always outside. Sports games and made-up games like Twilight Moonlight, a tag game where one group of kids would hide in the backyard of a house and another group would wait at the front steps, and yell, "Twilight, Moonlight, hope to see a ghost tonight," and then they would count down the hours, one o'clock, two o'clock, and so on until they screamed "MIDNIGHT" and tried to run all the way around the house and back to the safety of the front step without being tagged.

Don't suppose kids need that kind of thing anymore, Deputy Dan thought. Maybe because they live with the thought that the Anti Claus might be waiting for them in the dark backyard and tag them for good on Serial Killer Eve.

Or tag their mothers . . .

"Now you boys shouldn't run out in the street like that," Deputy Dan scolded a group of tykes who were dashing into the parade route to grab up candy that some of the characters on the floats were tossing. "You're liable to get run over. There will be plenty of other chances to get candy. Just be a little patient. There's enough for everyone."

Some things never change, he thought. They're still too young to really understand. They know a special visitor is going to bring something bad to town tonight, but they don't really understand, they don't know what his arrival is all about. They may know death to some degree, the expected, traditional deaths of grandparents and older relatives, but not the quick death brought by the Anti Claus. They don't know of the One Who Comes in through the Windows.

I got an early education in those areas, he thought. I may not have known that my mother had been killed, but I knew she was gone and I knew what it meant. For me the Anti Claus was never the mysterious, irresistible figure that he was for so many kids. I knew what he was all about early on. I didn't need any fairy-tale stories.

"No bike riding on the parade route, son. You'll have walk it or park it. Right now, okay?"

Well, I may not be able to bring her back, Deputy Dan thought, but I can bring back something approaching a normal life for the children of Standard Springs. It may be too late for the grownups; you get used to acting a certain way, you develop particular habits, and there's no changing you, even if your situation changes, even if what forced you into your state of mind gets locked away forever. Too late for them.

But for the children, it may be a different story. Take away the shadow of the serial killer now, and all this terror and dread might become a hazy, vaguely unpleasant memory for them, something that is seldom reflected on, something that does not dictate their way of life. Who knows what they will think of it in the years to come. They might even look back on these days with a certain fondness, as a time when the enemy was clearly known, and the town gathered together to celebrate that knowledge. Who knows what dangers might be lurking in the future.

Deputy Dan strode along with the parade, sometimes keeping pace, other times cutting back and forth across the street through the gaps, making steady but slow progress up Pain Lane. He began to feel a sense of anxiousness and excitement build as the blocks ticked away and the dispersal area came closer and closer.

He felt proud about the job he had done in apprehending what was very probably the serial killer. Of course, fate had sort of dropped the suspect into his net; Mrs. Flatwire, you could say, made a citizen's arrest on the man. She should get some of the credit, that was for sure.

It hadn't been easy, though, convincing Sheriff Eeha to hold the suspect for a few hours longer than necessary after the parade. The Sheriff was stuck in his ways, didn't like to rock the boat. But when the shark was hung up in your net and didn't have any more fight in him, then you had to move fast, because you might never again get such a sweet chance at him.

The more Deputy Dan thought about it, the more he grew convinced that their prisoner was the Anti Claus. Apart from his own investigations, Sheriff Eeha had shared with him what he had discovered in the stranger's notebook. If he had any doubts before, those rambling, nutszo writings were the clincher. Who else but a maniac would write stuff like that?

Now they had him, locked up in a cage at the front of the parade before thousands of witnesses. Even if he escaped somehow, the whole town would know that face, and he would never be able to sneak unseen into town again. From this day forward, their serial killer was a marked man.

Wait until the folks realize what's in store for them, he thought proudly. Just wait 'til they see.

Suddenly there was a commotion somewhere up the route, something that cut through the normal parade din, something that did not belong. There were cries, horses whinnying. Heads along the route turned to the north in a wave.

Deputy Dan began walking swiftly up the street, scanning the mass of bodies for trouble, but the floats and marchers were blocking his view. He broke into a run.

About a block ahead a knot of people were gathered along the left side of the road. Something was wrong; parades were usually such orderly affairs that the sight of people standing and kneeling in the street in a chaotic group was alarming. A man wearing a tall black cowboy hat with silver spangles was guiding a skittish chestnut stallion away from the scene.

Deputy Dan waded through the onlookers, who were all gazing at something on the ground in their midst. "Make room," he said. "Sheriff's Department. Official business. Make room, please."

"Somebody get an ambulance!" a woman called out.

Finally, the Deputy saw the source of the commotion. Rhea Quill, the first female member of the Standard Springs Fire Department, was crouched beside a prone dog. A human in a dog suit, actually, its trench coat askew and its big wet nose caved in on one side. The dog was breathing, but its tail was not wagging.

"What happened here?" asked the Deputy.

Glancing at the Deputy, Rhea said, "A horse bolted and trampled the poor guy. I don't think he even saw it coming."

"I'll call an ambulance," the Deputy said.

The dog stirred, rolling its shoulders forward, trying to sit up. "No, no need for an ambulance," said the dog. "It's just a little bump. I'll be fine."

"You really should have a doctor examine you," Rhea said. "You might have a concussion or something."

"The show must go on," said the dog.

"We've got medical personnel on call," the Deputy told the dog, "just for emergencies like this. It won't be a problem at all."

"Just got the wind knocked out of me," insisted the dog, sitting up.

"Are you feeling any pain in your limbs?" Rhea asked.

"No," the dog said, its head darting here and there. "Never felt better in my life, in fact."

"It's a miracle you didn't break your neck," she said.

"It *is* a miracle!" the dog exclaimed, abruptly popping up to its feet. Then its tail broke into wagging and it reached into its trench coat and handed Rhea a red lollipop. "Much obliged."

She smiled. "Thank you."

"By the way, my name is—"

"Okay, folks, the show's over!" Deputy Dan announced. "All you spectators get back on the curb. Those of you who are in the parade return to your places. Let's get this parade moving again. . . ."

●

The remainder of the Parade of Fear proceeded according to form, apart from a minor flood of blood in the streets when a storm drain got fouled up with confetti. Deputy Dan's next responsibility was to help make sure the parade broke up smoothly in the dispersal area and, more importantly, he thought, to take the Man in the Cage into custody and wait out the night.

By the time the Deputy reached the dispersal zone adjacent to Pain and Maple, now a jumble of floats and dark costumed figures, he saw Sheriff Eeha up on the Scream Queen float, releasing the prisoner from the cage. The Deputy hurried over and was waiting for them as they climbed down to the street. The Sheriff led the prisoner to a sheltered area at the rear of the float. The Deputy's heart began racing.

As Deputy Dan fumbled with the set of handcuffs attached to his belt, the Sheriff quietly told the stranger, "I have to admit it, you did some good work out there tonight. One of the best cage men we've ever had. I mean that sincerely."

"Thanks," said the man, shedding his prison oranges. "I tried to do my part."

"I hope we can get someone as good as you next year."

"N-N-Next year?" Deputy Dan said.

"Is that it?" asked the stranger, tugging a black baseball cap low over his eyes. "Can I go now?"

"Your debt has been paid," said the Sheriff. "You're a free man."

25

This is my most favorite place in the world," Debbie told her favorite poet as they walked down the path leading to Mrs. Toddler's pond. "I come here when I'm blue or need to think and it always makes me feel better." They sat down on the flat rock beside the dark, fragrant shore. Bullfrogs were trilling, and a bat flitted just above the surface of the water. Debbie had never visited the pond at such an odd hour and it was strange to see the water so dark, so mysterious.

"I told Mrs. Toddler I was going to build a house on a raft right in the middle of the pond. Oh, I wasn't really serious, but I sure like to think about it."

"This is a right pretty place," said Ole, leaning forward and dipping his fingers into the water. "Right pretty."

"There's a turtle who likes to sun himself right over there," Debbie said, pointing to a dead log jutting out from the water. "At first he used to dive into the water as soon as I came, but now he just sits there and looks at me with kind of a bored look. I see a muskrat once in a while, too, but he's still scared of me."

"I wrote a poem about a muskrat once," said Ole.

"That's right! You did! How did it go? Don't tell me! I know: 'Hey, I figured my brain's goofiness some special deal. I lay around like a lazy bum, my head burning something fierce. Boy, I was sure jealous of those devil-may-care animals—grinning caterpillars; muskrats, sleepin' like a kid in the sun.' "

"I never heard anybody read my poems aloud before," said Ole, looking at Debbie with a kind, shy smile. " 'Course, I read them to my hogs all the time. Works better if I can hear the words. If they squeal too loud, then I know I need to fix 'em up some."

"I didn't know that," said Debbie. "That's very interesting. I didn't know pigs . . . I didn't, well, you know what I mean."

"Hogs are very sensitive creatures. Did you ever notice their ears?"

"Not really, I guess."

"Big, sensitive ears they are. You put the wrong words together and it's like blowing a police whistle at a dog. They'll let you know right away that they don't approve."

"Do you miss them?"

"I surely do. I'm going to have to leave town very soon. I told my neighbor I'd be back by Sunday. He's got a threshing contest Sunday afternoon over in Nutterfield."

"Oh," Debbie said, her heart plummeting.

"What's the matter?"

"Well, I was wondering . . . can I visit you some time?"

"Sure thing, kiddo."

They sat by the pond, mostly not talking at all, and then toward morning, as the long night first began to give way to the new day, the sound of sirens disturbed their reverie. It was difficult to judge the distance, or direction, but they seemed to be not too far away.

"Well, I guess that's that," Debbie said.

"What do you mean?" Ole asked.

"The choice has been made. I hope it's nobody I know. Come on, let's go see. It's part of the ritual. Everybody does it." She offered Ole her hands, and helped him to his feet.

Together they wound down side streets and through vacant fields, following the cry of the sirens, and then following the crowds.

The center of attention on this early Sunday morning was a small, one-story yellow house located about four blocks west of Debbie's home. The Sheriff's car and an ambulance were parked on the lawn, red lights revolving. People in uniforms were going in and out of the house. She didn't recognize the house at first, until she heard someone say, "Poor Rhea. She was to be married next summer."

"My gosh," Debbie said, putting her hand to her mouth.

"Came right in through her bedroom window," someone else said. "That's what I heard."

Rhea. It must be Rhea Quill, Debbie thought with distress. She had demonstrated first-aid techniques for Debbie's health class just this past spring.

"Did you know her?" Ole asked.

"Not really. I knew who she was, though. Gosh, what a terrible thing to happen."

"Can I have your attention, please?" said the Mayor, who was standing by the yellow police tape with Samantha Sink, still dressed in her dark pageant gown. When the crowd quieted down, the Mayor said, "Thanks for coming this morning, folks. We've got a fine turnout. I'll try to make this short." He held up a pair of gleaming silver scissors for everyone to see, then passed them over to Samantha.

"I present to you our new Scream Queen, Samantha Sink!" said the Mayor. "Samantha? It's all yours!"

The new Queen nervously gazed at the police tape, holding the scissors in her right hand. She closed the scissors on the ribbon, but nothing happened. She drew the scissors back. Looking determined, she slipped the scissors around the tape again and snapped them shut. The tape broke, the two ends fluttering to the ground. The spectators applauded politely.

"Let's go," Debbie said, tugging at Ole's elbow, as the crowd advanced on the house.

"Is that it?" he asked, letting her pull him back into the darkness.

"That's enough," she replied.

26

The sun had not yet risen on Standard Springs the morning after, and the birds had just begun to sing outside the Mornings' still, white house, but Debbie was awake and busy. She paced the bedroom floor, her mind flipping wildly, nerves all jangled.

She wasn't afraid, but she was pretty darn close.

After all, it was her first time. . . .

•

Debbie packed some belongings into a knapsack and stepped lightly down the hall.

Going quietly downstairs, she left a folded sheet of paper on the kitchen table and headed for the back door where she had parked her bike. She hopped on and rode around the house and into the street.

It felt like any other day in Standard Springs.

Any other day.

Debbie went downtown first, stopping at the newspaper office. She folded a second sheet of paper in half and wrote on the outside: *"For Mr. Griff Grimes."* It's certainly not the best one ever, she thought, but it's a start. She opened the after-hours slot and slid it inside.

From there Debbie rode over to the corner of Vine and Bludgeon. There were no screams on Bludgeon Street this morning.

Molly was waiting on the front step, suitcase at her feet. Debbie glided toward her, leaving her bike on the lawn.

"Hi," Debbie said. "You look tired."

"Tired, yes," said Molly.

"It's over, for this year. He got Rhea Quill."

"I heard. I was friends with her. I talked to her about career stuff; she helped me a lot. I liked her a lot."

"I didn't realize . . ."

Molly attempted a smile. "Why don't we get going?" She got up, took her suitcase, and went over to her white convertible. Setting the bag in the backseat, she climbed into the car on the driver's side.

Debbie hesitated, gazing at the boy next door's house. Then she looked at the girl next door, who was watching her carefully.

"Let's go," Debbie said quickly, getting in on the passenger side, keeping her knapsack on her lap, hugging it tight. The car started up smoothly, and they headed down the street. The morning air was cool, the neighborhoods calm. The townspeople would be in their beds until noon, the one peaceful morning of the year. Tomorrow the countdown, the dread anticipation, would begin again.

It was only 364 days until the next Serial Killer Days.

"Where to?" Molly asked.

Yes, where to? Debbie wondered. We can go anywhere, she thought. Paristown, with Ole and his poems and his hogs. The Cities, with Jim Bowie and Latisha and the blue crystal. Maybe an island on some blue sea.

"Head north on County Ninety-nine," said Debbie. "I can drive if you're feeling tired."

"I am feeling beat," Molly said, "but I'm wide awake."

They drove by the high school and turned left at the hill, onto County 99, the Arrow Highway. As they reached the outskirts of town, neat houses and gardens replaced by the power station and cornfields, they saw a city truck parked at the edge of the ditch.

A worker along the roadside was busy pounding a green rectangular sign deep into the soil of her hometown. The Deputy stood nearby, head lowered.

The sign said: SERIAL KILLER, POPULATION 4,316.

Postscript

From the editorial page of the September 9 edition of the *Serial Killer Herald:*

We don't generally print poetry here at the *Herald.* Not that we have a grudge against it, but it's usually not news. This is different.

I got to know Debbie Morning a little bit in the days before she left town. A fine, brave girl. I thought I had something to teach her, but now I'm not so sure who learned more.

The fact is I've had this poem in my possession for several weeks, and I've been too big of a coward to run it. I could justify not printing it in all sorts of fancy ways, but my own fear is at the heart of the decision. Running it now may not serve the purpose she intended, and for that I apologize to her.

However, Debbie is the only one who will receive an apology regarding this matter. If you don't like it, you've got my number.

THE EDITOR

Heck, I Can't Be Ascared
by
Debra S. Morning

Sorry, folks, sorry, town, tried it all, tried the most.
Oh, I did every darn thing, every potion, every prayer, every
wound, every frightening thing.
Heck, I can't be ascared.
Not like you want me to, not like you want me to.
Don't think the worse of me, it's just not right for me.
Oh, the life I'm suited for, I don't know . . .
But it's something not like this.
I don't know what's to come of me,
I don't know where I will be,
Just some land where folks can't be ascared.